"What Do You Think Of The Sheriff's Office?"

Hunter asked as he showed Gaylynn around.

"Tack a few girlie posters on the wall and it would look just like your old tree house."

Hunter grinned at her tart comment. This was the Gaylynn he knew and loved.

Whoa there, he ordered his runaway thoughts. Love? Where had that come from? Falling for Gaylynn would be like eating gunpowder—you know it's going to detonate sooner or later.

But damn, she looked good in those jeans!

"Want to see my extra-heavy-duty handcuffs?" He tugged open the top drawer and dangled them in front of her.

"Can I use them on you?" she inquired.

Not trusting that fiendish gleam in her eye—was it caused by passion or anticipation of revenge for that gum in her hair all those years ago?—he heard himself promising, "Only if we're in bed."

"Cathie Linz's fun and lively romances are guaranteed to win readers' hearts! A shining star of the romance genre!"

—Susan Elizabeth Phillips

Dear Reader,

This month, we begin HOLIDAY HONEYMOONS, a wonderful new cross-line continuity series written by two of your favorites—Merline Lovelace and Carole Buck. The series begins in October with Merline's *Halloween Honeymoon*. Then, once a month right through February, look for holiday love stories by Merline and Carole—in Desire for November, Intimate Moments for December, back to Desire in January and concluding in Intimate Moments for Valentine's Day. Sound confusing? It's not—we'll keep you posted as the series continues…and I personally guarantee that these books are keepers!

And there are other goodies in store for you. Don't miss the fun as Cathie Linz's delightful series THREE WEDDINGS AND A GIFT continues with *Seducing Hunter*. And Lass Small's MAN OF THE MONTH, *The Texas Blue Norther*, is simply scrumptious.

Those of you who want an *ultrasensuous* love story need look no further than *The Sex Test* by Patty Salier. She's part of our WOMEN TO WATCH program highlighting brand-new writers. Warning: this book is HOT!

Readers who can't get enough of cowboys shouldn't miss Anne Marie Winston's *Rancher's Baby*. And if you're partial to a classic amnesia story (as I certainly am!), be sure to read Barbara McCauley's delectable *Midnight Bride*.

And, as always, I'm here to listen to you—so don't be afraid to write and tell me your thoughts about Desire!

Until next month,

Lucia Macro

Senior Editor

Please address questions and book requests to:
Silhouette Reader Service
U.S.: 3010 Walden Ave., P.O. Box 1325, Buffalo, NY 14269
Canadian: P.O. Box 609, Fort Erie, Ont. L2A 5X3

CATHIE LINZ
SEDUCING HUNTER

SILHOUETTE *Desire*®

Published by Silhouette Books

America's Publisher of Contemporary Romance

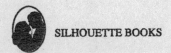

SILHOUETTE BOOKS

ISBN 0-373-76029-9

SEDUCING HUNTER

Copyright © 1996 by Cathie L. Baumgardner

Printed in U.S.A.

Books by Cathie Linz

Silhouette Desire

Change of Heart #408
A Friend in Need #443
As Good as Gold #484
Adam's Way #519
Smiles #575
Handyman #616
Smooth Sailing #665
Flirting with Trouble #722
Male Ordered Bride #761
Escapades #804
Midnight Ice #846
Bridal Blues #894
A Wife in Time #958
Michael's Baby #1023
Seducing Hunter #1029

Silhouette Romance

One of a Kind Marriage #1032

*Three Weddings and a Gift

CATHIE LINZ

left her career in a university law library to become a *USA Today* bestselling author of contemporary romances. She is the recipient of the highly coveted Storyteller of the Year Award given by *Romantic Times*, and was recently nominated for a Love and Laughter Career Achievement Award for the delightful humor in her books.

While Cathie often uses comic mishaps from her own trips as inspiration for her stories, she found the idea for this trilogy in her very own home—from an heirloom that has been in her family for generations. After traveling, Cathie is always glad to get back home to her family, her two cats, her trusty word processor and her hidden cache of Oreo cookies!

Special thanks to fellow crew members
Elainibonz and Ooopsie
for being at the other end of the modem
whenever I needed them!

One

"No!" Gaylynn Janos screamed. "No...don't!"

Sitting straight up in bed, Gaylynn blinked away the tears and dragged in ragged lungfuls of air. Her breathing remained unsteady as she tried to shake off the shrouds of the vivid nightmare she'd just had—a nightmare that was based on reality. She'd lived it all again—the reflective shimmer of the switchblade, the stark terror.

"It's okay," she whispered to herself, the sound of her shaking voice penetrating the silence in the otherwise empty cabin. "You're safe now."

Still trembling, Gaylynn reached out to check the time on her travel alarm resting on the bedside table. It was three o'clock. The muted daylight sneaking through the crack in the drapes told her it was afternoon. She'd been so tired after the fourteen-hour drive from Chicago to North Carolina that she'd fallen asleep on the bed while still fully dressed.

It probably would have been smarter to have overnighted along the way, but once she'd made the decision to come to her big brother Michael's secluded Blue Ridge Mountain cabin she hadn't wanted to stop until she'd reached its comforting safety. She'd hoped to leave the nightmares behind.

"No such luck," she muttered, scooting over to the edge of the bed and planting her feet firmly on the pine floor. The sound of her stomach growling reminded her of the fact that she'd gone to bed without eating.

She'd just finished making herself a quick salami sandwich from the food she'd brought with her when she caught sight of the cardboard carton Michael and his wife, Brett, had given her right before Gaylynn had left their wedding reception in Chicago the night before.

Balancing her lunch on top of the cardboard carton, Gaylynn carried everything outside to carefully plunk herself down on the large wooden rocking chair. Located on the sunny side of the covered front porch, the old-fashioned rocking chair was just begging for someone to occupy it. This was the kind of chair one could wile away the hours in, Gaylynn decided as she set aside the mystery package from her brother in favor of taking a bite out of her sandwich.

Spring came sooner this far south. At home the trees were still bare, but here they were proudly budding new leaves, creating a green tracery against the sky. A slight rustling in the underbrush got her attention. The noise was caused by a cat. A few seconds later two kittens skittered out. The feline family looked scared and hungry, *very* hungry.

Talking softly, Gaylynn removed some of the salami from her sandwich and, slowly going down the steps, offered it to the mama cat and her two kittens. Despite her careful movement, the animals were spooked and scurried back into the woods.

Gaylynn felt the sting of unexpected tears. She could empathize and *how*. She knew the feeling well. She was as spooked as those wild cats were. Scared to the bone. So frightened that the first thing you did was run, and ask questions later.

To her relief, she saw that the mother cat and her two kittens hadn't gone far into the woods. They were warily peering out at her. Kneeling down, Gaylynn quickly shredded the salami into bite-size pieces for them before leaving the meat in a spot where the cats could see and smell it.

Moving back to the front porch, she was glad to see the feline family eventually dash out and gulp down the food. The little calico kitten was the runt, and barely got a bite or two. The mother was very thin and appeared to be a Siamese. The other kitten was cream colored.

Once the food was gone, they all dashed back into the safety of the woods. They clearly felt safer away from people. At the moment, Gaylynn felt exactly the same way.

Sitting in the rocking chair, she absently picked up the cardboard carton her brother had given her, claiming it held "a little something from the Old Country to bring you luck."

Her big brother had never been one to believe in luck before, despite their shared Rom heritage. Her father, a Hungarian Rom, was another story, however. Konrad Janos had taught her many good-luck charms over the years. He'd even insisted she take his special rabbit's foot with her for this trip.

Her father couldn't know that there was no protection against the blind fear that welled up inside of Gaylynn. She hadn't told either of her parents what had really happened to her the month before. She'd just said she'd needed some time off from teaching in the inner city in Chicago. Since they'd never really approved of her working in such a rough neighborhood to begin with, they'd been too relieved at her decision to question her reasons for leaving.

Despite the warm sunshine, Gaylynn shivered as the mental images insistently flashed through her mind, the same images that had haunted her nightmare—the switchblade, the terror, the suddenness of it all. She'd had no warning of danger. No premonition of what was coming.

Sure there had been trouble at the school before, but she'd been known for her determination and toughness. She'd never had anything bad happen to her. She was well-liked and respected by her students. Even so, she'd never been foolish. She knew the dangers and had taken steps to avoid trouble. Until that day...

She'd stayed late at school. She'd been alone. Her mind had been on the school talent show when she'd felt arms grabbing her as she walked out of her fourth-grade classroom into the deserted hallway. Then the knife had been at her throat. No chance to scream. No chance to protect herself. She'd felt helpless. It wasn't a feeling she'd really ever experienced before. She'd always been the fearless one in her family.

Her assailant hadn't been much taller than she was, and at a little over five feet, she was no giant. But he'd been incredibly strong—due no doubt to the drugs he was high on, drug that had made him dangerously unpredictable, drugs that had turned a fourteen-year-old boy into a lethal stranger.

He'd wanted money. She'd given him what little she'd had. His hands shook. So had the long, shiny blade, pricking the smoothness of her skin and drawing blood. Gaylynn raised her hand to her throat, fingering the tiny scar that remained as she recalled the high-pitched desperation of his words.

Then it was over as suddenly as it had begun. He'd shoved her against the row of metal lockers and taken off. But for one brief moment she'd seen his face. Her assailant was Duane Washington. He'd been one of her students five years ago, one of the more promising ones. She'd had high hopes for him. Those were gone now. And so was he.

Twenty-four hours after she'd been held at knifepoint, Gaylynn had gone home and turned on the five-o'clock news to see the grizzly footage, the cameraman zooming in on the blood still darkening the street while the News team anchor's voice-over said, ''The suspect, Duane Washington, was wanted by the police on a mugging charge. He was fleeing, avoiding arrest, when he ran right into the path of an oncoming bus. Witnesses say that he died instantly.'' Another close-up, this time of a covered body being carried away. Duane's body.

The images still haunted her nightmares. The knife. The blood on the street. Duane's white-sheeted body.

Although the attack had happened almost a month ago, Gaylynn didn't feel she was recovering the way she should. She was still at the mercy of her emotions—primarily guilt and fear. Perhaps she'd done the wrong thing in calling the police and identifying Duane as her attacker. If she hadn't done that, he wouldn't have been fleeing and wouldn't have run right in front of that bus.

Then again, maybe if she'd been a better teacher, she would have seen signs much earlier that Duane was getting into trouble and she'd have been able to intervene before things had reached such a desperate point.

But there was no changing the past. The bottom line was that now Gaylynn, who had never feared traveling around the entire world on her own, was afraid to close her eyes in her own bed at night. She was paralyzed by fear—fear that she'd done the wrong thing, fear that she'd been in part to blame for Duane's death, fear that she'd been unable to protect herself, fear that she was so vulnerable to attack, fear that she'd be attacked again.

The counselor she'd seen had told her she was suffering from post-traumatic stress. Gaylynn expected it to go away, like the flu did. But her symptoms had remained. Unable to teach as she once had, she'd left, taken a leave of absence…until she was "her old self" again, as her principal had jovially put it.

The trembling overcame her as it did whenever she thought too long about what had happened. The rocking chair moved forward and the cardboard box on her lap almost slid off. Grabbing it, she moved the package closer to her body.

"You're safe now," she whispered, as she had every day since the attack. She had yet to learn how to *believe* it.

Taking a few deep breaths, she shoved her dark thoughts aside and instead focused on undoing the cardboard flaps to finally see what her brother had packed for her. Inside she saw an intricately engraved metal box along with a letter in a spidery handwriting.

Oldest Janos son, It is time for you to know the secret of our family and *bahtali*—this is magic that is good. But powerful. I am sending to you this box telling you for the legend. I am getting old and have no time or language for story's beginning, you must speak to parents for such. But know only this charmed box has powerful Rom magic to find love *where you look for it*. Use carefully and you will have much happiness. Use unwell and you will have trouble.

At the bottom of the letter was a yellow sticky note her brother had added. On it was written: "Thought you might find this interesting. Brett swears it worked in our case. Judge for yourself."

It was "the box," the one Gaylynn had heard so much about but had never seen before, the one Great-aunt Magda in Hungary had sent Michael. Three weeks later, he'd married Brett.

Gaylynn clearly remembered the first time she'd heard about the love-charmed box. It had been right before Christmas when her father had told the family legend of a beautiful young Gypsy girl who'd fallen in love with a nobleman who did not return her feelings. Gaylynn had promptly dubbed him the "no-account count."

The story was that the girl had paid to have a love spell cast on her behalf, but the old Gypsy woman who was in charge of such things had messed up the spell so that every second generation of Janos children would find love "where they *looked* for it"—which was taken literally! In remorse at her error, the old Gypsy had insisted the girl keep the engraved box she'd brought along, the only thing of value she had. Legend had it that the slightly out-of-whack love spell worked to this very day.

Leaning forward, Gaylynn tried to get a better look at the supposedly magical box—only to have the rocking chair shift forward, thereby tilting the box so that the lid opened.

Knowing the family legend that you'd find love with the first person of the opposite sex you saw after opening the box, Gaylynn automatically looked up— to see an old man dressed as a bum shuffling along the edge of the woods that surrounded the cabin.

Startled, she stood. The man disappeared back into the woods and the box lid flipped shut again.

"Great," she muttered. "When Michael looks up he sees beautiful Brett. When I look up I see a derelict moonshiner! Maybe this box *is* a curse instead of good magic." Having said that, Gaylynn carefully returned the box and the letter to the cardboard container. As she closed the cardboard flaps, she couldn't help wishing she could bundle up her own ragged emotions just as easily.

By that evening, Gaylynn had already named the family of stray cats. The mama was Cleo, short for Cleopatra. The cream-colored kitten turned out to be a cream-colored Siamese, complete with crossed eyes in a vivid blue color. She was dubbed Blue. The little calico kitten had the temporary nickname of Spook.

Gaylynn wandered down to the edge of the woods and fed them all the salami she had in the house, as well as a sampling of other fare—cheese crackers, skim milk, a can of tuna. Tomorrow she'd have to get some dried cat food from the little gas station/food store at the base of the mountain. And some more food for herself.

Looking up, she only now realized that night had fallen while she'd been engrossed with the feline family. Not long ago, she'd enjoyed darkness. Now the woods that had se   :d so peaceful became ominous, with the stark shapes of the foliage and trees taking on the outline of someone ready to strike.

Gaylynn jumped to her feet, her sudden movement scaring away little cross-eyed Blue, the only one who'd let her get within a foot. Now the kitten bolted, bringing tears to Gaylynn's eyes. Damn, she'd never been the weepy type before. She hadn't even cried when she'd broken her arm in two places at fourteen.

Biting her bottom lip to keep her unruly emotions at bay, Gaylynn quickly made her way back toward the cabin. Halfway there, a floodlight flickered on, illuminating her way. She remembered Michael telling her he'd installed a light-activated light.

She'd no sooner gotten inside the cabin when the sound of gravel crunching in the stillness of the night made her freeze in her tracks. Someone was outside!

Gaylynn couldn't help it. Fear washed over her.

The twin beams of a car's headlights pierced the shadowy darkness of the living room. The cabin was far enough off the beaten track to ensure that no one would just be passing by. That was one of the reasons Gaylynn liked it so much. Perched on the top of a hillside, it was just her, the kitties and the other wildlife, none of it human—other than the brief glimpse of that old moonshiner.

She was not expecting company. Only her family knew she was here. Yet a car was definitely making its way up the long and narrow gravel driveway—a driveway that was private and so secluded no one could stumble upon it by accident.

Silently thanking her brother's foresight in installing the large floodlight on the outside corner of the cabin, Gaylynn tiptoed to the front door and peeked out the curtained window. The driveway was brightly lit. There was a car all right. A dark-colored sedan. She didn't recognize it.

The car door opened and she saw a man step out. The floodlight shone down on his head. He had dark hair. As he turned toward the cabin she saw his face clearly for the first time.

An instant later, her fear was replaced by anger. Yanking the door open, Gaylynn confronted the man climbing the wooden steps leading up to the front porch.

"What are *you* doing here?" she demanded.

"Now is that any way to greet an old friend?" Hunter Davis returned with a slow smile.

Two

Gaylynn hadn't seen Hunter Davis in ten years, but in many ways it was as if she'd only seen him yesterday. His dark hair was longer than she remembered and had a touch of silver at the temples. His deep-set eyes were exactly as she remembered, a vivid shade of green—the color of backlit spring leaves.

"Aren't you going to invite me in, Red?" he drawled.

She'd hated the nickname as a kid, and she intensely disliked it now. Hunter had given her the nickname when, as an awestruck thirteen-year-old, Gaylynn had used henna on her hair to impress the "only man in the universe" for her. Hunter hadn't known that *he* was that man. He'd been eighteen, five years older than her. In her idolizing eyes, he'd seemed like the perfect man.

Seeing Hunter now, she realized how wrong she'd been. *Now* he was a man. Not perfect perhaps, but definitely rather awesome. The years had honed him to a sharp edge, as was illustrated by the fine lines at the outer edge of his green eyes. His level brows intensified his elemental attractiveness. His face was too powerful to be handsome, yet it held a woman's attention longer than any surface good looks would.

When, at age thirteen, Gaylynn's plain brown hair had turned a vivid red as a result of her henna experiment, Hunter had started calling her Red. She'd tagged after him and her brother, anyway. She'd fallen in LOVE—with capital letters and all the fervor of a teenager.

And when Hunter had gotten married at twenty-five, she'd shed a tear or two. It was the last time she'd cried. Until last month.

"What are you doing here, Hunter?" she asked.

Instead of answering, he eyed her with a frown. "What's wrong?" he said bluntly. "You look awful."

Her cheeks burned. She knew her clothes were rumpled, and her jeans had dirt marks at the knees where she'd bent down to feed the stray cats. She'd planned on taking a shower after she'd eaten her late lunch, but had gotten distracted. Her hair hadn't been brushed in hours and probably had a twig or two sticking out of it from her exploratory walk along the edge of the woods. "I wasn't expecting company right now. Go away," she muttered with self-conscious irritability, trying to move him toward the front door. "Come back later."

She might as well have tried to move Mount McKinley. "I'm not going anyplace until you tell me what's wrong."

"Nothing's wrong. I'm on vacation, okay? This is the way I look when I'm on vacation. If you don't like it you can leave!" Her famous Hungarian temper flared as she stomped off to the bathroom and slammed the door. Looking in the mirror, she saw that he was right. She did look awful. After washing her face and brushing her hair, she put on some lipstick before opening the door.

Of course, Hunter was waiting right outside, just as she'd known he would.

"There, is that better?" she asked, complete with a mocking pirouette.

"I wasn't talking about your hair. I was talking about your eyes."

"I didn't get a lot of sleep..."

"That's not it," he interrupted her. Taking her chin between his fingers, he tilted her face up. "There's something about the expression in your eyes..."

She closed them. Tight. But that only made the feel of his warm fingers on her skin all the more powerful. In an instant it was as if she were thirteen and in the throes of her ardent crush on him all over again. Her world became centered on the point of contact between them. Heat traveled from his fingertips to her skin, racing to her heart. Her senses were in a turmoil as he practiced his black magic on her with nothing more than the merest brush of his hand.

Disconcerted, she snapped her eyes open and stepped back from him. "Did Michael send you over here to check up on me?"

"He told me you were coming."

"I'll shoot him."

"Now hold on..."

She wanted to hold on, all right. She wanted to hold on to Hunter's broad shoulders, wrap her arms around him and never let go. Great. This was *not* the time for her to remember the stupid crush she'd had on him. This was the time to get rid of him. Before she said or did something foolish.

"I'm fine. You don't have to waste any more time checking up on your friend's nuisance sister."

"You're not a nuisance."

"That's not what you used to say."

"You were five years old then."

"Nine," she corrected him, remembering the very day his family had moved in next door. At first she'd hero-worshipped him... then she'd fallen for him. "What exactly did my brother say when he called you to come check up on me?"

"It wasn't like that. He was just warning me that someone—you—would be using the cabin for a while. I've kind of been looking after the place."

"You don't mean you've been staying here, do you?" she asked, horrified by the image of sharing the compact cabin with him.

"No, of course not."

"Good."

"I've got my own place a stone's throw away."

"Stone's throw?"

He nodded. "You can't see it from here, but it's just over the ridge there. About a two-minute walk from here."

"Great." A two-minute walk from temptation. Wonderful.

"Michael didn't tell you that we went in together right after our academy days to buy this property and the two cabins on it?"

"No, he didn't tell me." The rat.

"So how about you? Are you going to tell me what's happened?"

"Nothing has happened. Well, that's not exactly true. Michael and Brett got married yesterday. Actually, it was the second time they got married, it's kind of a complicated story," she noted dryly. Made more so by a Gypsy love-charmed box, which was sitting in a cardboard container next to the couch at this very minute.

Too bad Hunter couldn't have been the first man she'd seen when she'd opened that box. Unlike Michael, who'd been the practical one in the family, Gaylynn liked to think there was some magic in the world.

At least, she always had in the past. Now she wasn't so sure. About anything.

"Yeah, I know about the wedding," Hunter was saying. "I was sorry I couldn't make it, but I was working."

Gaylynn nodded. She knew he worked as a police officer. In fact, Hunter and Michael had gone to the police academy together. Her brother hadn't finished the program, preferring to work on his own in the world of corporate security. But Hunter had graduated near the top of his class and been hired as one of Chicago's finest. He'd looked dashing in his uniform and had been considered the ultimate bachelor, dating a number of women over the next few years. Then he'd up and gotten married the month Gaylynn had started college.

"So how's your wife doing?" she asked with forced cheerfulness.

"I haven't got the faintest idea. We were divorced almost five years ago."

The news took her by complete surprise. "Michael never told me you were divorced."

Hunter shrugged. The action focused her attention on his broad shoulders. He wore a denim shirt with jeans that were a shade darker. Both had seen their share of washings, making them soft enough to conform to every line of his body—molding his shoulders and narrow hips.

"Down girl," she muttered to herself under her breath.

"What did you say?"

"Nothing. I was just talking to myself."

"That comes from spending too much time alone."

"No, you don't understand. I came up here to do just that. To be alone. It's what I need right now."

Hunter watched the nervous slide of her fingers through her straight hair. Gaylynn had never been the fidgety type, even as a kid. She'd been the gutsy type. Fearless. Hell, he still remembered the time she'd invaded the tree house he and Michael had built in the only tree in the Janos's postage-stamp backyard. Gaylynn had only been nine or so at the time, a mere baby compared to his advanced age of fourteen. But she'd climbed the dangling rope that supplied the only entry to their tree house, this despite the fact that she wasn't wild about heights. She'd ended up with bloody hands from the rope burn she'd gotten. He knew she still had the scar between her thumb and index finger—her badge of courage, she liked to call it in the old days.

She'd changed from those days. Somehow he'd always pictured her in his mind as she'd been as a coltish teenager. Now he was confronted with a woman, a very attractive albeit untidy woman. He got the strangest feeling when he looked at her...

"Why are you staring at me like that?" Gaylynn demanded uneasily.

"I was just thinking about that time you invited yourself to our secret tree house. Do you remember?"

"Yes." Gaylynn stared down at her hand, the one with the tiny scar, the one with her badge of courage. It was still there, mocking her fear. Now she had another scar, the tiny one at the base of her throat from the knife, as well as the jagged one on her soul.

She'd lost more than the thirteen dollars and twenty-one cents she'd had in her wallet that day she'd been attacked. She'd lost her nerve.

It hadn't happened instantly. At the time, one of her first concerns had been making sure that no one in the police department blabbed to her brother, who still had a few police connections from his academy days. Driving home that night after the attack, she'd resolutely blocked the entire thing out of her mind. At first, she thought she'd succeeded.

Then she'd seen the TV news. The horror had gripped her by the throat and the tears had started. She'd gritted her teeth and gone back to work the next morning only to have the terror creep up on her the moment she'd entered her classroom. She hadn't been able to speak, hadn't been able to move. For the first time in her life, Gaylynn had experienced the paralyzing effects of blinding fear.

Unaware of her thoughts, Hunter was saying, "You weren't afraid of anything in those days." The approval in his drawl was clear.

She knew he valued courage. She just wished she had some. But she did have her pride. She didn't want him seeing how scared she was; she didn't want his sympathy or pity. She had to get rid of him. "While I'd love to talk over old times with you, I was just getting ready to make dinner..."

"Great. I haven't eaten yet."

"I don't have enough food for two."

"Then we can go to my place. I've got plenty of food."

She shook her head vehemently. "I don't want to go out."

"Fine. I'll bring the food over here. I haven't seen you in years. It'll be fun to catch up on things."

Kissing him would be fun. The rebel thought chased through her mind. She chased it out just as fast. What was wrong with her? She didn't have enough problems already with all her nightmares and no backbone? Now she had to go and get sentimental about a man she had a crush on years ago? A man who had always treated her like a sister.

"I make a mean spaghetti sauce," Hunter declared, his Southern drawl seductively sliding down her spine.

"I'll bet you do. But—"

"I'll be right back with all the fixings."

Hunter was gone before she could voice a protest.

The good news was that he'd left before she'd made too big a fool of herself. The bad news was that he'd be back and she'd better be ready for him. The problem was that Gaylynn had her doubts that there was any way for her to get ready for a man who represented even more danger to her already shattered peace of mind.

Hunter had only planned on doing a quick check on Gaylynn and then going on his way. He didn't know what had made him insist on sharing his dinner with her. Maybe it had been the shadows in her big brown eyes—root-beer-colored eyes that he'd remembered as always sparkling with life. Of course, a lot of time had gone by since then.

She had to be what . . . nearing thirty by now. He'd just turned thirty-five himself. Hunter didn't know where the time went. He'd meant to keep in better touch with Michael up in Chicago, but all he'd been able to manage was a Christmas card most years. He really regretted not being able to attend the wedding.

He also regretted blurting out his concern so awkwardly, telling Gaylynn she looked awful. That wasn't like him. He didn't blame her for almost biting his head off. But he'd seen the shuttered pain and had wanted to help.

What could have caused this change in Gaylynn? Why had she left her brother's wedding reception last night to head for a remote cabin in the mountains? Michael, too wrapped up in his newfound happiness, hadn't had any answers. But Hunter planned on getting answers, because he couldn't help her until he did.

And I suppose the fact that she's an attractive woman has nothing to do with your Good Samaritan routine, an inner voice mocked him.

"She wasn't *that* attractive," he muttered under his breath as he entered his own cabin.

Right, now you're talking to yourself, just like Gaylynn was. And if she isn't that attractive, then why did you feel such a zip of excitement when you looked at her?

"That was hunger," he said as he grabbed the fixings for a great spaghetti sauce from his cupboards and fridge.

Gaylynn was just the sister of an old friend, and his reasons for wanting to make sure she was okay were strictly altruistic. That was his story and he was sticking to it, as he and Michael used to say.

Gaylynn spent the first ten minutes after Hunter had left getting cleaned up. A quick shower and change of clothing helped. There wasn't time to wash her hair, but a vigorous brushing had improved things somewhat. Her baby-fine brown hair was straight as a board and had a definite mind of its own. The blunt-cut tips ended just past her shoulders. It was getting too long; she should have gotten it cut.

Hunter's hair had been long, too. Like he'd been too busy to have it cut lately. She hadn't been too busy, she'd been too freaked out.

Biting her bottom lip, she took a deep breath and reapplied her makeup. "You're a good actress," she told her reflection in the mirror. "So put on a good act tonight."

Granted, she'd been able to sidestep Hunter's questions so far, but he wasn't liable to let her off the hook so easily next time. Like a dog with a bone, Hunter would just nag at her until he found out what was wrong. He was like her brother that way.

Luckily for Gaylynn, Michael had been distracted by events in his own life at the time of the attack on her. He'd been fighting to keep custody of little Hope, who'd been abandoned and left with Brett before she and Michael had gotten married. Yes, her brother had had his hands full, which was the only reason he hadn't given her his customary third degree about her wanting to use his cabin. Instead, he'd just let her do her thing.

That wouldn't be the case with Hunter. So she'd better have her story down pat by the time he came back because he could sniff out a mystery a mile away.

"Okay, I admit it, you do make a mean spaghetti sauce," Gaylynn admitted as she licked a stray bit of sauce from the corner of her mouth.

Hunter watched her with the eyes of a hawk. She'd noticed the way he'd been watching her all evening, but she was unable to discern the thoughts going through his head. For her part, she'd been deliberately cheerful, talking about some of the people from their old neighborhood.

"I can't believe little Joey del Greco is a priest now," Hunter said with a rueful shake of his head.

Gaylynn grinned. "I'll tell him you said so."

"Last time I saw him, he was what we call down here 'knee-high to a grasshopper' and was stealing apples from the Jablonskis' apple tree."

"The apple tree is gone, and so are the Jablonskis."

"Funny how you picture things staying the way they were when you saw them last. Like you. I pictured you with that White Sox cap on your head."

"I still wear it on bad hair days," she declared dryly. "How about your folks? How are they doing?"

"Fine. They've retired down to Florida now. Have a nice condo in Sarasota."

"Does your dad still claim the Cubs are gonna win the World Series before the year 2000?"

"He sure does," Hunter confirmed with a slow smile. "Although I've got to say that he's starting to get a little nervous about that prediction. And how about your folks? Your dad still making those Gypsy weather forecasts that amazed the entire neighbor-hood?''

"You bet. He's more accurate than any of the weathermen on TV.''

"I remember one time he took Michael and me fishing up in Wisconsin and tried to teach us how to 'tickle' trout. Neither one of us managed to *catch* on, though.''

Groaning at his obvious pun, Gaylynn crumpled up her paper napkin and tossed it at him.

Hunter merely grinned and ducked before continuing his story. "Your dad caught something like half a dozen trout. And I'll never forget the way he left one hanging in the tree nearby before we left.''

"To bring good luck and ensure there would be good fishing at that site the next time,'' Gaylynn explained.

"That's right. You know, I've got to tell you, I was always envious of the way you guys got to open your Christmas presents early on Christmas Eve. And if I remember right, you got extra presents even earlier than that.''

Gaylynn nodded. "Left in our shoes on Saint Nicholas's Day.''

"We had some good times in those days.''

"Yeah, we did,'' she agreed softly. When she'd been a child, the world had been her oyster. She'd been the only girl in her family, with one older and one younger brother. Their protective presence had seen her through life's rough spots. Until now. This was one rough patch she was going to have to make it through on her own. She didn't want them knowing how weak she was; she didn't want to disappoint them.

If Hunter saw how spooked she was, he'd tell them. Spooked. That reminded her to ask Hunter about the feline family. "Listen, I meant to ask you before if you know someone who might have lost a Siamese cat and her two kittens. I saw them in the woods earlier today and gave them some food."

Hunter shook his head. "Haven't heard of anyone in this area missing their cat. Chances are they are strays."

"They need looking after."

So do you, Hunter wanted to say. Gaylynn had shoved more pasta around her dish than she'd actually eaten. Did she think he wouldn't notice? Did she think he was buying her restless cheerfulness as the real thing? If so, she had a lot to learn.

"You never did tell me why you decided to come to Michael's cabin," he prompted her.

"I already told you, I needed a vacation."

"So you're on spring break from school?"

"Not exactly."

"Then what exactly?"

"You're nosy, you know that?"

"Hey, I'll have you know that my interrogation techniques have been honed to a fine art. You might as well tell me all your secrets now," he stated with a lazy grin as he helped her stack the dirty dishes on the table. "I'll get them out of you sooner or later."

"Oh, no, Officer Davis." She gasped mockingly, putting one hand to her heart. "Not your dreaded tickling routine!" Hunter might not have learned how to tickle trout but he'd excelled at tickling her in their childhood days. "Anything but that!"

"So you're willing to confess now?"

"You've got me." She sighed, putting a dramatic hand to her forehead. "I'm an escaped felon, wanted by the city of Chicago for two overdue parking notices. I'll give myself up peaceably," she added, holding both her hands out to him. "Cuff me now and take me away."

"Don't tempt me," he muttered, disturbed by the sudden sexy image of her wearing handcuffs and little else. What was wrong with him? She was Michael's kid sister, for heaven's sake!

"Then stop making such a big deal about this," she said in exasperation. "I needed some time off from my teaching position so I took a vacation. End of story."

"How long are you staying?"

"I'm not sure."

"When is your vacation up? Wait a minute, now that I think about it, teachers can't just up and take vacation during the school term."

"Bravo, Sherlock."

"Which means you're what...on some kind of leave or something?"

"That's right."

"A medical leave?"

His persistence was irritating her. "That's none of your business," she said, taking the dishes from him and transferring them to the stainless-steel sink.

Hunter followed her into the open L-shaped kitchen to say, "Meaning I'm right."

"No, meaning it's none of your business," she stated. "Look, I've been teaching for seven years in a stressful situation. It's not surprising that I got burned out. End of story."

"Someone like you doesn't get burn out."

"What do you mean 'someone like me'?" she demanded.

"You've got too much determination to burn out. Besides, you're too damn stubborn to give up."

"What makes you think you know anything about me? You haven't even seen me in ten years."

"I've kept track of what you've been doing. Michael would brag about you in his Christmas cards, saying that you insisted on teaching where you were needed and could make the most difference, despite the fact that he and the rest of your family didn't approve of you working in such a bad part of the city."

Having said that, he reached around her to put a dish in the sink. She felt his body heat against her back, felt his arm brush her breast and she jumped as if hit by lightning.

"What's wrong?" he asked, confused by her startled-cat routine. "Why did you jerk away from me like that?" Then, as one possible explanation hit him, his expression turned serious, bordering almost on alarmed. "Oh, my God.... Were you sexually assaulted?"

Three

"**D**on't be ridiculous. I was *not* sexually assaulted. Just because I'm a little jumpy doesn't mean that anything like that happened to me!" Gaylynn said.

"And even if it had, you wouldn't tell me, would you?" Hunter retorted.

"If you think that, then why ask me in the first place?"

"Because I'm trying to figure out how I can help you."

His words were like tiny arrows piercing her pride.

Lifting her chin, Gaylynn stated, "I don't need you to help me. I'm not one of those injured baby birds you used to take in when we were kids."

"I'm still pretty good at mending broken wings," he murmured, coming so close behind her that his breath stirred her hair and awakened silent yearnings.

Hunter was pretty good at *plenty* of things, not least of which was making Gaylynn feel like a young girl on her first date—filled with anticipation of what could be.

Curtly reminding herself that she was no young girl, Gaylynn squelched her wistful thoughts before they took further flight. "I'm sure the birds around here are glad to hear that you're good at mending their broken wings," she replied dryly. "But I don't have wings and I don't need your help."

Gently brushing her shoulder blades with his finger-tips, Hunter softly said, "Remember how Michael told you that these would grow into angel's wings when you got older?"

"I was a gullible kid," she admitted.

"And now? Are you still gullible now?"

"Sometimes," she replied, stepping away from the magnetic temptation of his touch. "After all, I let you come over and badger me tonight, didn't I?"

"You forgot to mention the delicious meal I made. Tomorrow night, *you* can cook."

"Hey, I didn't come to the mountains to cook," she protested.

"Why did you come here?"

But she was on to his tactics now. "I've already answered that question several times. Maybe you need to get your hearing tested," she mockingly suggested. "How old are you now? Almost forty?"

Hunter did not look amused. "I'm thirty-five and you damn well know it."

His arrogant assumption that she would know his age irritated her. "Forgive me if I've been too busy living life to recall all the details of yours."

"Yeah, I heard about you living life, traipsing all over the globe."

She relaxed. This was something she felt more comfortable talking about. "That's right. During my summer breaks I used to travel a lot," she reminisced fondly. "I've been elephant-trekking in Thailand, slept on the beach in Morocco, shopped in Singapore, gotten rained on in England's Lake District and visited the rain forest in Costa Rica."

"You *used* to be a globe-trotter?"

"Yeah, well, now I stick a little closer to home."

"Any reason for that?"

"Finances, and the fact that although I've seen a lot of the world there are still plenty of places right here in America that I haven't seen yet. The Blue Ridge Mountains, for example. This is my first time down here."

"Then you'll have to be sure and drive along the Blue Ridge Parkway. We could do that this weekend. I'm off-duty—"

"I don't need to go anywhere else," she interrupted him. "I can see mountains from here."

"There are even more spectacular views to be seen."

"I'll be fine right here."

"If I didn't know better, I'd say that you're hiding away up here."

That was exactly what she planned on doing, and she didn't aim on having Hunter get in her way, regardless of how sexy she might still find him. His shaggy hair had just a touch of gray at the temples while his piercing green eyes reflected an interrogating intensity. She could easily picture Hunter as the embodiment of a gray wolf. He was certainly a natural born predator, trained to go after what he wanted and to get what he went after. She had to remind herself that all he wanted from her was the truth, but even that was too much for her to give him right now.

Seeing she wasn't about to unload her innermost thoughts to him, Hunter chose a more nonthreatening topic. "So how's the rest of your family doing?"

"Fine. Dylan flew in for the wedding." If her rolling-stone younger brother hadn't planned on flying out the morning after the reception, Gaylynn might have put off coming down to the mountains for a day or two. She hadn't seen Dylan in a year.

"So what's he been up to lately? Has he taken over your globe-trotting ways?"

"He pretty much sticks to the western United States, but he certainly doesn't stay in one place very long. He been working the rodeo circuit out there as a saddle bronc rider. He's even won a couple of championships. And did you hear that Michael and Brett have adopted a baby girl, Hope? She's adorable. Smart, too. Naturally I'm her favorite aunt."

"Naturally. Did she tell you that?"

"She's not actually talking a lot yet. She's a little over nine months old and is just about ready to walk on her own. I brought a picture of her." Gaylynn retrieved a pocket-size photo album from her purse.

"You brought *a* photo?" Hunter said dryly. "Looks more like an entire book full to me."

"Yes, but see how adorable she is?" Gaylynn's expressive voice reflected her excitement as she showed him a series of pictures. "Isn't she the cutest baby you ever saw?"

Hunter nodded accordingly. "I'm surprised you left her behind. They grow fast at that age, don't they?"

"Yeah, they do," she agreed wistfully.

"You know, I expected you to have a family of your own by now."

"I could say the same about you."

"Being a cop is hard on family life. I moved down here in the first place because my wife, Tricia, had a hard time with my being on the force in Chicago. I thought it would be easier on her if I worked for the county sheriff's department down here. The danger involved with the job is certainly less here in a rural area than it was in the city."

"But there is still danger?"

He just shrugged. "Life is dangerous. But it wasn't just the danger that torpedoed and sunk my marriage, it was the fact that my ex-wife hated living here. Said she was going crazy in this backwater hole-in-the-wall. Last I heard, she'd moved back up to Chicago and married a plumber."

"Sounds to me like you're well rid of her. You never did have the best taste in women," she told him bluntly. "Remember that redheaded bimbo you went steady with in high school? Sindy spelled with an *S*."

"I wasn't dating her for her spelling skills."

"That was obvious."

"I'm surprised you remember her."

"A chest like that is hard to forget. I was convinced she stuffed her bras with helium balloons. That was the only memorable thing about her. But I'm sure you've forgotten a lot about the old days."

"I didn't forget you."

"Yeah, right. I treasured all the cards and letters you sent me over the years," she said mockingly.

This time his shrug was just a tinge self-conscious. "You know I'm no good about things like that."

He'd been married by then, so Gaylynn hadn't expected to hear from him. Hadn't *wanted* to hear from him. She'd wanted to forget him, and she'd succeeded for the most part.

Okay, so maybe a tiny part of her *had* compared all the men she'd dated with Hunter, and none of the city guys had quite stacked up when compared to Hunter's rugged strength. But she hadn't been unhappy with her life. Far from it.

And then her life had crumbled like a butter cookie, leaving her crumbs instead of substance.

Her sudden yawn scattered her dark thoughts.

"I guess that's my signal to go and let you get some sleep," Hunter noted wryly.

"Sorry," she muttered, belatedly putting one hand to her mouth. "It's not the company. I'm just tired."

"I can see that."

"Thanks for stopping by tonight, but I'll be fine. Really."

"I know you will," Hunter told her. What he didn't tell her was that the reason he knew she'd be fine was because he planned on sticking around and making sure she stayed that way.

That night Gaylynn's dreams were spun around a wolf blending into the woods surrounding the cabin. A wolf with Hunter's leaf green eyes. She was dressed as Little Red Riding Hood, complete with red cape and hood. She woke up at the part where the wolf was in bed, seductively coaxing her to join him.

"In your dreams," she muttered as she got out of bed and headed for the shower. No way would Hunter try and coax her into bed, unless she was sick . . . and then his intentions wouldn't be romantic but practical.

The shower helped to clear the cobwebs from her mind. There was a nip in the air this morning, so she tugged on an aqua-colored sweater over top of her white T-shirt. Her jeans still had dirt marks on the knees, so she opted for a pair of black denims. There was no washer in the cabin, so she'd have to see if there was a Laundromat in town.

After the kitties finished the last of her canned tuna fish, Gaylynn bit the bullet and made a long list of things to stock up on. She didn't want to be making the twenty-minute trip down the mountain any more often than was absolutely necessary. Not because she was intimidated by the rather harrowing drive on the narrow gravel road. Even the equally narrow one-way bridge that forded what the nearby sign proclaimed to be the Bitty River didn't bother her—despite the fact that the chipped cement on the corners attested to the fact that more than one run-in had already occurred on that bridge. No, she didn't want to be making the trip very often because she just didn't feel like mingling with civilization yet.

As Gaylynn pulled in front of the compact building that housed "The Pit Stop Filling Station—Filling You And Your Car," she realized that this might not quite qualify as civilization, per se.

The building was brick and resembled the filling stations of the forties. The pumps still had round glass tops, and a sign over the door advertised the virtues of a motor product that hadn't been made in at least a quarter of a century.

In front of and across half the open threshold lay some sort of animal—large and lumpy and an auburn color—forming an unusual oversize and bumpy welcome mat. On closer inspection, she realized the animal was a bloodhound.

"He don't bite and neither do I," a voice boomed from inside. "Dog's lazier than a hibernating bear. That ain't his name a'course. His last name's Regard. First name is Bo. Which makes him Bo Regard. Just step on over him."

Gaylynn did, rather gingerly. The bloodhound responded by lifting its head, all of an inch, before letting it drop again with a muffled thump. "You've got a big dog there."

"Oh, he don't belong to us. He just comes visiting every day. Must be my scintillating conversation skills. Yer a sight for sore eyes."

Startled, Gaylynn said, "Excuse me?"

"Now, don't you mind him none," an older woman stated as she stepped out from behind the counter. "Floyd here says that to every woman under the age of a hundred who walks through that door. My name's Bessie. Bessie Twitty. And that grumpy-looking, talkative man over there is my husband, Floyd. And you must be the sister of Hunter's friend. From up north, aren't you?"

Gaylynn nodded, not even stopping to wonder how Bessie knew who she was already. "From Chicago."

Bessie grimaced, making her wizened face look even more wrinkled. "I hate cities."

"You never been in one," Floyd retorted.

"Have so. I been up to Knoxville one time. Didn't care for it atall." Bessie said the words together, as if they were one.

"And my eyes *are* sore," Floyd declared. "That's why I have Bessie doing my post-office chores."

"Did you come in to get some stamps for post-cards?" Bessie asked Gaylynn. "We don't get many tourists in these parts, so I don't have much call for postcard stamps."

"Unless it's Ma Battle entering one of those dog-gone contests of hers," Floyd inserted.

"I do declare that woman gets more mail than everyone else in town put together," Bessie said. "How many postcard stamps will you be needing, then? I'm sorry, I didn't catch your name, dear."

"It's Gaylynn and I don't need any stamps."

"You didn't get any gas-o-leen," Floyd said, enunciating it as if the word consisted of three separate parts.

"I came to stock up on some food," Gaylynn stated.

"The Piggly-Wiggly over in Summerville is where most folks do their stocking up," Floyd replied.

"How far away is that?"

"About a forty-minute drive," Floyd said.

"An hour, if you obey the speed limits," Bessie inserted.

"I was driving these roads before they *had* speed limits," Floyd said.

"I'd rather not go that far away," Gaylynn decided. "I'll just get what I need here."

"We don't have the best selection," Bessie had to confess.

"But we do have something of just about everything," Floyd added.

"Just not much," Bessie tacked on.

"And we don't carry any of them fancy TV dinners, neither."

"We have lots of ice cream, though."

Gaylynn was getting a crick in her neck from turning her head back and forth between Bessie and Floyd. A conversation with the two of them was like a tennis match, short words volleying back and forth.

"What about tuna? And cat food?" Gaylynn asked.

"I reckon we can fix you up with something. You bring some kitties down from the city with you?"

"Actually, I found a family, a mama and two kittens, up in the woods. I was wondering if they belonged to anyone around here?"

"Not that I know of. Most likely they're just strays. We get lots of those down here."

Yeah, and I'm one of them, Gaylynn thought to herself. She gathered up her groceries, many things she hadn't eaten in years—including oatmeal from the round cardboard box instead of a microwaveable packet. The bread they had was fresh baked by someone in town and the strawberry jam was homemade. She bought as many cans of tuna and boxes of dry cat food as they stocked. The Pit Stop didn't have any fancy paper bags for her purchases, which made her glad she'd brought along a cloth tote bag to lug the stuff back to her car.

But first she had to step over Bo Regard again, who this time lifted his head all of *two* inches before letting it drop again. He had a face only a mother could love and was actually so homely he was kind of cute—even if he did drool.

As she loaded her trunk, she heard the telltale rush and ripple of the river. When driving in early yesterday morning, she remembered noticing that the buildings in Lonesome Gap clung to the small ribbon of land between the two-lane blacktop road and the river.

Beyond that were the mountains, lush and green, rising directly beyond the narrow valley floor.

Gaylynn might have lingered longer were it not for the Twittys' curious stares as they watched her out the Pit Stop's front window—their noses plastered against the plate-glass right beneath the neon Gas sign. With their eyes on her, she managed to spill half the contents of the tote bag before she got everything in the car.

Gaylynn didn't realize how uptight she was until she pulled in front of her brother's cabin. Only then did the tension ease from her shoulders.

She spent most of her afternoon coaxing the kittens to let her pet them after they'd gobbled down their food. Spook still kept her distance, so that Gaylynn couldn't even tell if she *really* was a she. But Blue did let Gaylynn briefly brush her fingertips over the kitten's back. Gaylynn was reminded of Hunter touching her own back—with a similarly soothing movement.

Once Hunter was in her thoughts, it was real tough booting him back out again. The best she could do was relegate him to a back corner of her mind as she sat on the covered front porch and watched the feline family playing with leaves left from last autumn.

At first, she didn't even realize she'd picked up a pencil and started doodling on the back of the old-fashioned receipt from the Pit Stop. Looking down, she was amazed to discover that she'd drawn the view of the woods in front of her. Even more surprising was the fact that it wasn't half-bad.

Funny, she'd never been able to draw worth a hoot before. Her artistic abilities were somewhere between zilch and nada. It had been something of a joke at the school, where she'd had the crookedest display boards of any class. The kids were better at art than she was.

There was a lot she missed about teaching—the feeling of making a difference, the interaction with the kids, the expression in her students' eyes when they first grasped a new concept in reading or math. For the first time in a long time the thought of teaching didn't fill her with blind panic. She wasn't ready to return yet, not by any means, but she could feel the peaceful surroundings beginning to work their magic on her.

Thinking of magic naturally led her thoughts to the Rom box she still had stored inside the cabin. And from there, her thoughts roved right on to Hunter. Would he stop by tonight as he'd said he would? Tomorrow *you* can cook dinner, he'd told her last night. She'd told him not to bother, but she had the feeling that he took her words about as seriously as he did learning how to tickle trout.

The sun was just about setting, and from her vantage point she could see the heavenly orange glow radiating from the western horizon. Hunter should be coming home from work soon.

As it turned out, Hunter didn't stop by that night so he couldn't sample the tuna-and-noodle casserole she'd made. In fact, he didn't come home at all—at least, she hadn't heard him drive up by the time she'd fallen asleep at almost 4:00 a.m.

The next morning, she'd woken up with the birds and taken a walk, not deliberately intending to head in the direction of his cabin. Her feet just took her there on automatic pilot, even though she'd never been to his place before. The cabin's design matched the one she was staying in, with the addition of a stone chimney on one side.

Hunter's car wasn't in front and there was no one home. She tried not to worry about him, reminding herself that he'd been taking care of himself just fine for years now.

But the questions came, anyway. What if something had happened to him? Had there been trouble at work? Was he all right? She knew it wasn't logical to be worried about him. As he'd said, this wasn't Chicago—drive-by shootings were not a fact of life in Lonesome Gap.

Her fingers trembled as she fed the kitties back near her cabin. How would she know if something had happened to Hunter? There was no phone in the cabin and she hadn't given him the number on the cellular phone her brother insisted she bring with her. Who would know to contact her?

Stop it, she told herself. Nothing has happened to him. Geez, what a sissy you are! Talk about a nervous Nellie!

Her anxiety only served to remind Gaylynn that she was in no condition to be able to cope with the danger involved with his life, and she hated being so weak. Hunter deserved someone as strong as he was.

Gaylynn had just stepped out of the shower when there was a knock at the cabin's front door. Her heart leapt to her throat.

"Gaylynn, it's me," Hunter loudly announced from the other side of the door.

Forgetting that she was still wearing her rose-colored terry-cloth robe, she rushed to the door and opened it. Hunter looked haggard and weary. "Sorry I wasn't able to take you up on that dinner invitation last night."

"No big deal," she lied. "It wasn't really an invitation, at all. In fact, you invited yourself and then I un-invited you."

"Yeah, well, there was some trouble in town."

"What happened—were you hurt?" She ran the two questions together.

"Some idiot in a pickup truck decided to take a joy-ride down the main highway. On the wrong side of the street. Playing chicken with a semi-truck filled with fertilizer. Both vehicles swerved—luckily in opposite directions—to avoid an accident. As it was, the pickup ended in a ditch and the semi-trailer tipped over. After making sure the driver of the semi was okay, my deputy approached the pickup—only to end up with a bullet through his foot."

"He was shot!"

Hunter nodded.

"Will he be okay?"

"He'll live," Hunter replied as he lowered himself to the lumpy couch. "Considering where he could have been shot, he's mighty lucky."

"You don't sound very sympathetic."

"I'm not. I spent the night doing the rest of his shift and then my own."

"It's not his fault he was shot!"

"It sure was."

"Excuse me?"

"I said it's his own fault he got shot. Who else's would it be?"

"The man who shot him."

"Exactly."

"So did you arrest the man who shot him?"

"Don't think I wasn't damn tempted to."

"You mean you let him go?"

"He's at the clinic over in Summerville."

"And then he'll be arrested?"

"Unfortunately, stupidity isn't against the law."

"You let the driver of that pickup go?"

"Of course not. He's locked up awaiting transferal to the county facility."

"But you just said—"

"Deputy Carberry shot himself," Hunter explained. "He was approaching the pickup truck and getting ready to withdraw his weapon from his holster when he tripped over something in the grass. His finger squeezed the trigger and, presto, he shot himself in his big toe. Damn fool wasn't wearing his regulation shoes. By the time I got to him he was bleeding a lot, but it looked worse than it was."

Bleeding a lot. Gaylynn paled at the words.

"You don't look too good," Hunter noted in concern. "You're not going to pass out on me or anything, are you?" he demanded, getting up to put an arm around her and gently tug her against his broad chest.

With the contact, her sensitized nerve endings absolutely tingled. She could feel the heat radiating from his body. He was wearing his sheriff's uniform—such as it was. A black leather jacket, blue shirt and black pants. The wide belt around his trim waist held official-looking things like handcuffs, bullet cases and a flashlight holder. Now that she looked closer, she realized the pants were actually black jeans. And they fit him to a T.

Stop it, she told herself, angry with herself for falling prey to her own emotions for him. Emotions that were from the past, not her present, she reminded herself.

"You're shaking," he declared in disbelief. Looking down at her through narrowed eyes, he said, "This reaction has something to do with what happened to you, doesn't it?"

"I don't want to talk about it."

"You might as well tell me, I'll hound the truth out of you one way or another."

Furious, Gaylynn said, "What gives you the right—"

Hunter interrupted her to say, "This does." And then he kissed her.

Four

Hunter only meant to show her that he wasn't going to let her escape from the truth anymore. That she couldn't escape from him.

Gaylynn only wanted to teach him that he couldn't browbeat her into doing his bidding anymore. That she wasn't an adoring teenager ready to obey his every command.

But once his lips covered hers, she could fight no longer. His tender fierceness and hunger took her completely by surprise.

He showed her how much he wanted her.

She taught him that she wanted him, too.

His lips were firm yet soft as he moved his mouth over hers, deepening the kiss and taking it from the initial stage of experimentation to one of heated pleasure. Did she part her lips because of the seductively coaxing darts of his tongue or because of her own need for him? Who cared? She only knew she couldn't get enough of the minty male taste of him.

He drew her closer. His hands rested on her shoulders, conveying not just their physical warmth but a sense of assurance and leashed power. Fighting never entered her mind. Only surrendering did. And in doing so, to be victorious. Conquering indecision, she put her arms around his neck and leaned even farther into the kiss.

He tightened his hands on her shoulders, tugging her closer for one soul-searing, darkly devouring moment before suddenly setting her away from him.

Stunned, Gaylynn could only blink myopically at him—her mind a complete blank, her senses buzzing on full alert, her heart beating a mile a minute.

She lifted her trembling hand to her mouth, still quivering from the passion of their kiss. "What did you do that for?" Her question came out as a rusty whisper.

She'd spoken without thinking, and had meant why had he stopped kissing her, why had he so abruptly pushed her away. Thank God he took it to mean why had he kissed her in the first place.

"That wasn't planned," he muttered roughly, shoving one hand through his hair. "I was just trying to teach you a lesson—"

He got no further. "Don't bother," she interrupted him, her voice fiery enough to sizzle bacon. So he'd only kissed her to teach her a lesson, had he? Of all the nerve! The entire thing had been what... an act? His hunger had been a ploy, or maybe she'd just imagined it, projecting her own feelings on to him.

"I was just trying to get you to talk to me, to tell me what's been bothering you..."

So kissing her had simply been his way of getting the truth out of her. If so, he was successful. But the truth he got was that she was still attracted to him. "Your methods stink!" she exclaimed, tightening the belt on her robe.

Her anger didn't faze Hunter. Gaylynn spit like a kitten saying, "Stay away from me," when it really meant, "Don't hurt me."

"You can trust me," he softly reassured her.

"Yeah, your actions certainly proved that," she retorted sarcastically.

The disappointment she saw in his green eyes was the straw that broke the camel's back. She couldn't fight any longer. Because now she had something else to fear. And that was her growing feelings for him.

If she'd opened that love-charmed Rom box and immediately seen Hunter, she could possibly excuse the way she felt. This way she couldn't even blame magic. She didn't even have that justification.

She'd revealed too much of herself with that kiss. Revealed too much of her newfound need for him.

The best she could hope for was that once his curiosity about what was bothering her was satisfied, Hunter would move on. Oh, he'd offer his support first. And she'd accept it. On the surface. Because if she didn't, he might take it into his head to kiss her again. And while half of her wanted that desperately, the other half was afraid.

If Hunter really knew how utterly terrified she was inside, he'd go running in the other direction. No, she silently amended. Hunter had never been one to abandon a creature in pain. He'd try to mend her, like those birds he'd taken in as a kid.

So what should she do? What did anyone do when placed between a rock and hard place? Her best bet would be to tell him the truth and hope for the best. And to avoid looking in his eyes, she reminded herself while nervously twisting a strand of her hair around her index finger, practically strangling it in the process.

Taking her hand in his, Hunter squeezed it reassuringly. "Just tell me."

"Look, it... Before I can tell you, I want your solemn promise that you won't tell my brother or anyone else." Seeing that he was about to protest, she yanked her hand away and glared at him, forgetting her decision of not looking in his eyes made mere seconds ago. Her anger helped firm her wobbly backbone. "I mean it."

"Okay."

"Promise," she persisted.

"I promise."

"It's just..." She shoved her hair behind one ear before rushing on. "Something happened at school. I was mugged by one of my former students. It was my fault..."

"Your fault that you got mugged?"

"I was in the building late, later than I ever was. It was stupid. There had been some trouble before—we're talking about an inner-city school here. Not that it was awful by any means. It's just that you learned to take certain precautions. I didn't take those precautions that afternoon."

"Were you hurt?" he immediately asked.

She rubbed the tiny scar at her throat even as she shook her head. "Not really, no. He held a knife on me—he was just a kid, high on drugs. I didn't know what he'd do. I gave him all the money I had and he took off. I recognized him as he ran away. I called the police—''

''Then how come Michael doesn't know?'' he interrupted her to ask.

''Because I made sure the police didn't tell him. My brother had enough problems of his own at the time. He didn't need to be worrying about me.''

''Someone should,'' Hunter muttered.

She glared at him.

''All right. All right,'' he relented, holding both his hands out to indicate he'd hold his tongue, for the time being. ''Go on. Did they catch the kid?''

''He…he was killed the next day. I came home from work and saw it … on the TV. He was fleeing on foot, the police were after him, and he ran right in front of a bus. He died instantly.'' Gaylynn couldn't say any more. Couldn't talk about all the blood. Couldn't bear the flash of memory.

''And you've been trying to deal with all this on your own?'' Hunter demanded.

''No, I knew when I started crying and wasn't able to stop that I needed some help. I went to see a counselor afterward. Logically, I know all the reasons why I feel the way I do. I just need some time to heal.''

''And that's why you came here?''

She nodded.

''It was stupid of you to try and handle this alone,'' he said with characteristic bluntness. ''You should have told your family and your friends.''

She bristled at his ''big brother'' tone of voice. ''My roommate in Chicago knows what happened. I share an apartment with her near Lincoln Park. I had to explain why I was taking off for a few weeks. Before I left, I paid my portion of the rent through the end of the school year, when our lease is up. I had things all under control until you showed up." And kissed me senseless, a tiny inner voice continued in her head. "Everything will be okay once I've had some time to rest and recover. I've been teaching for seven years now. I probably needed the break. Maybe this is fate's way of making sure I get it."

Eyeing her closely, he said, "You're not thinking you're in any way to blame for that kid's death, are you?"

"What makes you say that?"

"I know you."

"Not as well as you think," she retorted.

"Maybe not," he allowed. "But well enough to know that you're the kind of woman who'd grieve for any loss of life, let alone someone who had been one of your students. Michael always grumbled about how you'd put in extra hours, use your own money to get supplies, take the time to make the kids feel important."

"They *are* important. Children are our hope for the future. In answer to your question, I know that, strictly speaking, I wasn't responsible for Duane's death." Emotionally speaking was another thing; she refused to confess her secret guilt, the secret fear that if she'd done something differently, if she hadn't stayed late that day at school, Duane Washington might still be alive today. That was a reality she was still trying to cope with. The police had told her that if *she* hadn't reported Duane, someone else would have. Her mugging hadn't been his first criminal offense. "I just wish I could have done something to have prevented it." That much was definitely true. "But you know how I am. Tough. I'll be back in the teaching harness again before too long." She said the words automatically, wanting to reassure him, wanting to make sure that he stopped worrying about her. "I just need a break for now. Time to relax, enjoy the peacefulness of the mountains, maybe do some sketching."

"I didn't know you sketched."

"*I* didn't know I sketched," she stated wryly. "I've never been able to before. Maybe I just lacked the inspiration. Goodness knows, there's enough beauty around here to inspire anyone."

"You've got that right," he agreed, but he looked at her as he said it.

Gaylynn nervously shoved her hair away from her face. She wasn't herself at the moment. She felt totally emotionally exposed. That's why she'd clung to him like plastic wrap. "I guess you could say that I'm not the fearless one in the family anymore," she acknowledged with ragged ruefulness, before ending in a whisper, "I'm not sure who I am anymore."

Hunter knew who she was, and it was up to him to show her that she was a very special woman. He didn't tell her so, knowing she wouldn't believe the words. He could see the vulnerability she was trying so desperately to hide, the underlying raw fear. No, mere words wouldn't cut it. He had to *show* her how exceptional she was.

In fact, he was still discovering just how exceptional—the kiss they'd just shared had shaken him, but good! No longer could he dismiss his coming to her emotional rescue simply because she was Michael's sister. The feel of her pliant mouth beneath his had wiped that fallacy clear off the map. His feelings for her were much more than just platonic. They were direct, intense and passionate. Attraction, chemistry, sex, lust—whatever label he put on it, friendship had nothing to do with it.

But Hunter also knew that Gaylynn had spent all of her life in a big city, or traveling to exotic and exciting locations around the world. None of those adjectives fit a quiet out-of-the-way place like Lonesome Gap. Sure, Gaylynn was hurting right now, but she'd get over that. He'd make sure of it. And when she did, when she was back to her old don't-mess-with-me self, she'd go back to her life in Chicago. That was a given.

Besides, he didn't exactly have a great track record where women were concerned. His own marriage had broken up because of the demands of his job and because of the isolation of living out in the boonies. In the intervening time since then, he'd made it a point to keep his relationships with the opposite sex on a superficial level. But there was nothing superficial about Gaylynn....

The bottom line was that Hunter had to help Gaylynn get her life back. And to do that, he needed to coax her down off the mountain.

It took Hunter two weeks to get his plans together. During that time he tried coaxing, bullying and teasing Gaylynn off the mountain.

It didn't work. She patted his cheek and sent him on his way, told him she was perfectly happy. And she *was* looking better than she had when she'd first arrived. But that spark wasn't back yet.

Never one to back away from a challenge, Hunter had no intention of giving up. With that thought in mind, he tried out plan B. Actually, he was probably on plan M or N by now, but who was counting?

She answered his knock on her front door faster than he expected. She was wearing jeans and a lace-trimmed sweater in a pale peach. The sweater's short sleeves showed off the light tan she'd gotten since coming to the mountains. The screen door added a blurred edge to her appearance, giving her a softly romantic look. In that instant, his heart leapt, as if he was seeing her for the very first time and his body was recognizing hers as its intended mate.

His intense man-to-woman reaction caught him by surprise and merely confirmed his earlier realization that his feelings for Gaylynn were not merely platonic. They weren't *merely* anything. They were powerful and vibrant, unexpected and unknown.

"Something wrong?" she asked him with a frown. "You look like you've been poleaxed."

"Picking up some of our mountain speech, are you?"

She wished she could imitate his sexy drawl, but there was no way. The Southern accent wasn't too thick; it was just right, complementing the natural flow of his voice.

"What can I do for you?" she asked him.

The image of her lying naked in his arms suddenly filled his head like a two-story screen at a drive-in movie. In living Technicolor.

"Hunter . . . ?" she prompted him.

"Uh, it's a beautiful day today."

"Yes, it is," she agreed. "You stopped by just to tell me that?"

"I've stopped by for our date."

She frowned in confusion.

"You didn't forget what day today is, did you?" he asked.

"Of course not. It's, uh . . ."

He could see her trying to remember.

Closing her eyes and wrinkling her nose for a second of concentration, she snapped her fingers and said, "It's April first!"

"April Fools' Day."

"Great. Does that mean I'm going to have to check to see if you've somehow short-sheeted my bed?"

"What?" The image of her and bed together was enough to momentarily short-circuit his thought processes as that two-story-high mental image of her filled the screen of his brain once again.

"You and Michael and Dylan used to play the worst tricks on me," she was saying. "Don't you remember? Putting food coloring on cotton balls and sticking them in the faucet filter fittings of the sink so the water came out all blue? My mom nearly had a heart attack when she saw my face."

The force of his attraction to Gaylynn was enough to give *him* a heart attack! All she'd done was smile in reminiscence and his blood pressure nearly shot through the roof. Stuffing his hands in his jeans pockets, he rocked back on his heels, reminding himself that his mission was to get Gaylynn out of her shell, not out of her clothing and into his bed.

"Yeah, well . . ." He cleared his throat and started again. "Are you sure I can't convince you to come with me for a drive along the Blue Ridge Parkway today?"

"You've asked me that every day off you've had since I've been here and my answer is the same. Thanks, but no thanks."

"Okay. Then come on." He took her hand and gently tugged her outside.

"Wait a second," she protested. "I said I didn't want to go on a drive with you."

"I know. I heard you. We're not going on a drive. We're going on a walk."

"A walk? Where?" she inquired wryly as he hustled her up a narrow path. "Clear up to West Virginia?"

"Gee, and you used to be such a trusting soul."

"Yeah, and I got rewarded by you and Michael stranding me up in that tree house for an entire day."

"It was only an hour. It just felt like an entire day."

It took Gaylynn a moment to realize that she could have said she'd been a trusting soul until she'd gotten attacked, but that *hadn't* been the first thing that had come to her mind, thank heavens.

Yes, she'd definitely done the right thing coming to the mountains the way she had. With the sun shining down on her bare head and the sound of bird song filling the air, it was one of those magical moments when it felt good just to be alive.

"So where are we going?" she asked him.

"I told you. For a walk. There are some things I want to show you."

He kept her hand in his, twining his strong fingers through hers. His touch didn't inspire a bolt of awareness. Instead, it created a magical warmth that spiraled along her arm to her very heart. Unable to resist, she tightened her hold and was rewarded for her boldness by him grinning at her over his shoulder before squeezing her hand in return.

The footpath through the woods followed the incline of a ravine, along a tiny creek, and was so narrow at first that they had to proceed in single file, with their clasped hands providing the physical bridge.

Blooming redbud and dogwood trees created a splash of pink and white against the spring greens.

"They say that in these mountains in spring, there must be as many words for green as the Inuit have for snow," Hunter said.

"I believe it," she murmured.

Lacking their full foliage, the trees filtered rather than blocked out the sunlight, allowing wildflowers to flourish. The forest bed was filled with them. And not just one or two single flowers, but entire beds carpeting the ground. Anemone, bellflower and violets were the only ones she recognized. There were many others she didn't. "What a lovely flower," she said, pointing to one in particular. "You wouldn't happen to know what it's called, would you?" she asked Hunter.

Turning to look at her over his shoulder, he glanced at the flower before grinning wickedly. "It's called *trillium erectum.*"

Gaylynn almost choked. "Very funny! If you didn't know you could just have said so, instead of making something up."

"I'm telling you, it's a *trillium erectum.*"

"Right. And I suppose that one next to it is *trillium orgasm?* Never mind—" Using her free hand, she put her hand over his mouth. She could feel his smile branded into the heart of her palm. "Don't tell me. *Trillium erectum,*" she muttered with a shake of her head.

The teasing swirl of his tongue darting into her palm reminded her that she still had her hand over his mouth. She yanked it away.

"Anything else you want to know?" Hunter asked with a look of devilish innocence.

"I should have known better than to ask you anything on April Fools' Day," she stated.

"I'm not kidding you about the name of that flower. Look it up in any wildflower book."

"Since when have you been an expert on wildflowers?"

"Since I found out there was one with a name like that," he replied with a slow smile and that lazy drawl of his. "Makes a big impression on the ladies."

"Now I see why mothers warned their daughters about men who led them down the garden path," Gaylynn noted wryly.

"You want to turn back?" His look was a challenge she wasn't about to resist.

"No way. Lead on."

They hiked on for about twenty minutes before Gaylynn called a halt. "Time out!" she gasped.

"Just two more feet and you'll get a view that'll make everything worth your while," he promised her.

"Two more inches and I'm taking a rest stop," she declared.

"Never holler whoa in a mud hole," he told her.

"Which means what?"

"When things are getting rough, that's not the time to stop and give in. It's the time to keep moving on, pushing forward."

"I would push forward, but there's a man the size of a mountain in front of me," she noted, placing the palm of her free hand in the small of his back and giving him a gentle shove. "You're blocking my view."

Truth was, he *was* the view—she'd spent the past twenty minutes watching his lanky stride with decidedly feminine approval. He had the long, surefooted walk of a born woodsman.

The view two feet away, when they reached it, was indeed worth the walk. So was the view of Hunter's denim-clad backside, she silently noted with a grin.

Seeing it, Hunter said, "Ah, you like, huh?"

"I like very much," she agreed sassily before turning to study the scenery laid out before her.

The sky was an intense blue, bluer than she'd ever seen it in Chicago. Laid out before her were row after row of shadowy blue mountains, the color unique to this area and unlike anything she'd seen elsewhere in her world travels. It was a sea of flowing curves, with every ridge separated from its sisters by deep and narrow ravines. There was only mountain and forest for as far as the eye could see.

"I've often found that a little height makes a sight of difference in the way a body sees things," Hunter told her in a soft mountain drawl.

"You've got that right," she agreed, her voice touched with awe at the mind-boggling vista. There was something mystical about the way the mountain ridges blurred one into the other—the closest being the darkest, and the farthest the lightest, with infinite shades in between. She counted eight different layers fading off into the distance.

She didn't realize she'd counted aloud until Hunter said, "The Cherokee have a story about how these mountains were created. They say that at one time the earth was wet and soft and very flat when Great Buzzard flew over the land. He'd been sent on a scouting mission and had flown a long way when he reached this area. By then he'd grown weary and his wings struck the mud. That's how the valleys were formed. On each upbeat of his wings, a mountain was raised."

"Since then, these mountains have seen a lot of sorrow," she murmured. "Especially for the Cherokee. They lived here for a thousand years until Andrew Jackson became president and decided they were in the way. Gold had been discovered nearby, so he had thousands of Cherokee herded up at gunpoint and then forced them to march on the Trail of Tears all the way to Oklahoma."

"Some Cherokee did manage to stay here and survive," Hunter said. "My great-grandmother was two-thirds Cherokee from the Qualla Reservation just south of the Great Smoky Mountains National Park."

"I didn't know you had Cherokee blood."

"I'm told I have my great-grandmother's nose," he told her with a grin. "Ended up getting me in several fights over the years. Of course, my Irish heritage no doubt also contributed to my being labeled a hothead in school. That was one of the politer terms used."

"Irish, huh? So that's where you get your gift of blarney from?"

"My mother's maiden name is O'Brien," he acknowledged. "Her favorite thing about Chicago was the fact that they knew how to celebrate Saint Patrick's Day by dying the Chicago River green."

"They still do," Gaylynn said. "They use vegetable dye, similar to you dying our tap water blue on April Fools' Day."

"Well, I don't have any tricks up my sleeve this April Fools' Day," he told her, undoing both sleeves of his denim shirt to show her his arms.

"Yes, well..." She blinked away the all-too-tempting image of those strong arms holding her. "Umm, we'd better be heading back down."

But she hadn't taken more than a dozen steps when she had to stop. "Ow!"

"What's wrong?" Hunter immediately asked in concern, taking her by the elbow and helping her over to sit on a fallen log a few steps away.

"I've just got a rock or something in my shoe," she noted in disgust while undoing the laces on her left athletic shoe.

Relieved that nothing serious was wrong, Hunter sat beside her on the fallen log. He watched as she propped her ankle on her opposite knee and tugged off her shoe. They were in the forest once again, surrounded by greenery, the panoramic mountain view now hidden.

A sudden piercing shrieking nearby startled Gaylynn, who was somewhat precariously perched on the log to begin with. She flinched and almost ended up on her fanny in the ferns. Instead, she somehow ended up in Hunter's arms, pressed against him. His arm around her waist safely anchored her to his chest.

"What was that?" she asked breathlessly.

"A jay."

"Oh." Feeling foolish, Gaylynn went to pull away. She only made it far enough to look into his eyes and then she was hooked.

Five

Hunter's hands cupped her arms as he lowered his head for a kiss that started out light and infinitely gentle before slowly progressing at a delightful pace, the rhythm accelerating into a warm cadence. Where their first kiss two weeks before had been like being struck by lightning, this one was like being immersed in a warm sensual pool. There was no sense of rushing, but his restraint only served to increase her craving for him even more.

When she nibbled at his bottom lip, he growled his approval and their kiss blossomed into an equal exchange of parted lips, sleek tongues and husky murmurs. Using the tip of his tongue, he stroked the roof of her mouth, the feathery caress making her shiver with excitement as she moved even closer.

Hunter did the same, tugging her into his arms. Her breasts were pressed against his chest. He used one arm to clamp her to his side, which left the other free to cup her cheek. The warm slide of his fingers into her hair created a rush of desire within her. While kissing her, he stroked his thumb against her jawline. Every new touch was a potent discovery of just how powerful his effect was on her.

The need grew and with it so did the intimacy of both their kiss and their embrace. She put her arms around his back and met each thrust of his tongue with moist approval. Moments later she was lying halfway across his lap, her pelvis in intimate electric contact with his.

She'd just felt the full force of his arousal when their kiss was abruptly broken off as they both almost fell off the log!

Gaylynn immediately scrambled to her feet before remembering she was only wearing one shoe. Looking down, she gazed into Hunter's face, his eyes lit with sultry laughter.

"Now I know where that phrase 'as easy as falling off a log,' comes from," Hunter noted with a rueful laugh.

Easy? Gaylynn thought. Yes, it would be all too easy for her to fall in love with Hunter. She was halfway there already. Halfway to heartache. Why couldn't she have fallen for him when she'd had her act together, when she'd been strong enough to fight for him, to fight for his love? When she'd been deserving of him.

He might have found their situation funny, but she didn't.

"Timing is everything," she muttered under her breath before briskly heading down the path ... back to reality.

* * *

"Good, Blue!" Gaylynn exclaimed as the cream Siamese kitten pounced on the string that Gaylynn was pulling across the porch floor. "You clever kitty!"

During the past two weeks she'd managed to get the feline family as far as the cabin porch. Spook still preferred to hide out under the porch, while Cleo kept a watchful eye on both her kittens from the steps.

Blue, meanwhile, was keeping her watchful eyes on the string. She missed just as often as she caught it, perhaps because of her crossed eyes, Gaylynn wasn't sure. She only knew that she felt fiercely protective of Blue, Spook and Cleo. She'd even fixed them a little bed out of the cardboard carton her brother had put the Rom box in.

Which left the love charm out in the open, sitting on the table at the end of the lumpy couch inside the cabin, and very much on her mind.

When Blue curled up on her lap, Gaylynn spent the next hour reading through some of the papers she'd found stuffed in the carton with the box.

They were notes, in her mother's flowing handwriting, recording the family legend as told by Gaylynn's paternal grandmother, who'd died long before she was born. According to family legend, those who had trouble with the charmed box that would "find love where you look for it" included one ancestor who tried to sell the box, and was soon thereafter struck by lightning in a freak storm.

"So it's definitely not a good idea to try and pawn this thing," Gaylynn murmured, rubbing Blue's ear with one hand while she held the notes in the other.

Her mother had written as a postscript:

No one knows exactly how old the charmed box is, time is not measured by the Rom—aka Gypsies—in the same way it is with others. I have tied some stories to world events, such as the American Revolution in the late 1700s, to try and pinpoint them. In that era, care was not taken with the opening of the box and a Gypsy man fell in love with a woman who was already married. She fell for him, as well, and their love ended tragically, with them both committing suicide at the hunting lodge of her husband.

"Avoid hunting lodges and married men," Gaylynn muttered. "And all of this trouble because an ancestor of mine fell in love with a no-account count who didn't return her feelings. Yeah, I know how that feels, Blue," she informed the kitten, who was kneading her little paws in ecstasy. "Unrequited love is the pits. But that's no reason to go and have a love spell cast. And it wasn't even a *good* love spell at that, but a messed-up one, that skips a generation."
She read some more from the notes.

The box has also brought good fortune, as was the case with the Gypsy man who fell in love with an Austrian countess. Together they did much to ease the harassment of the Gypsies who traveled in their jurisdiction.
Another story tells of the Gypsy woman who fell in love with the most powerful man in their tribe, even though he was twice her age.
Legend has it that the box once actually stopped a feud, when the son of one tribe saw a young woman from their rival tribe and both fell in love. Their union brought the two tribes together.

"I wonder if that first Gypsy girl ever got the no-account count she was in love with?" Gaylynn murmured aloud, but she couldn't find any answer to her question in the notes her mother had written.

Careful not to disturb Blue, who was now sound asleep on her lap, or Spook, who had crept underneath the rocking chair, Gaylynn reached down for the charmed box itself, which she'd brought out on the porch with her.

Her finger tingled as she touched the warm metal. Most likely that was caused by the fact that the box had been sitting in the sun. This was the first time she'd taken the opportunity to study the box closely. The intricate engraving on the lid depicted a scene that included palm trees and a sailing ship.

"Which means what?" she wondered aloud. "That I'm about to take a long sea voyage?"

There were four crescent moons on the left corner of the lid while a streaking sun setting over a line of mountains adorned the right corner.

"Or maybe it means that I was meant to come to the mountains?"

The sides of the box were also engraved with hearts, moons, stars and what looked like an honest-to-goodness wizard! "Cool," she murmured, impressed by the detailed workmanship.

Opening the box, she remembered to look for the silver key her brother had told her was inside. But she found no key. Instead, there was a medallion of some kind. The red-and-white ribbons were old and faded. As she touched them with her fingertip, she was filled with a strange sort of calm strength.

Holding the medallion in one hand, she looked through her mother's notes again but found no reference to any medals, or to what the box contained at all, for that matter. As Blue woke up, and had a playful interest in the ribbons, Gaylynn decided it might be safer to return the medallion to the box for the time being.

She'd learned a lot that afternoon. She'd hoped that the supposed love charm only worked on a *nonattached* person of the opposite sex, but instead had found that wasn't necessarily the case. Married or single, older or younger, it didn't matter. The love charm zapped and the rest was history. Which left her praying that the old moonshiner she'd seen that first day hadn't gotten mystically smitten. That's all she'd need right now.

"Don't let the fact that you've been waiting all your life for this moment make you nervous," Hunter teasingly told Gaylynn.

"Shut up and let me shoot," she retorted.

"I thought we were playing a little friendly one-on-one here. Nothing serious."

"Speak for yourself." Taking a deep breath, she focused her attention on the net before shooting. The basketball bounced against the backboard and rolled halfway around the rim before dropping in. "Yes!" she shouted triumphantly.

"This isn't the NBA play-offs, you know."

"You're just mad because I'm beating you."

"You are not *beating* me! So you're ahead a few points . . ."

"Ten points, to be exact."

When Hunter had shown up this afternoon, Gaylynn hadn't been too keen on his suggestion that she come to his place to shoot a few hoops. Actually, he'd

downright challenged her to a little one-on-one, goad-
ing her into it, taunting her with the memory of how
Michael and Hunter had never let her play with them.

"Here's your chance to play with me all you want,"
Hunter had murmured.

At the time, she'd wondered if Hunter could possibly have meant that comment to be as provocatively
tempting as it had sounded. Probably not.

Her height, or lack thereof, gave her a definite dis-
advantage in this game. Hunter was a good eight or
nine inches taller than she was. But she had good eye-
hand coordination and speed, plus the advantage of
distraction.

It started with her taking off her zippered jacket to
reveal the formfitting purple tank top she wore underneath it, a top that left a good four-inch section around
her waist bare above the waistband of her black span-
dex leggings.

She'd hadn't dressed this way on purpose, she'd been
doing her exercises when he'd shown up at her door-
step. But she certainly made good use of her somewhat scanty attire, once she noticed his attention
wandering in that direction. She'd bump into him every
so often and run her hand down his sides.

"Foul!" Hunter cried as she tried the maneuver
again.

"No way!" she returned. "Come on, Hunter, I've
seen fourth-graders play a better game than you."
Having said that, she proceeded to steal the ball from
him.

"Yeah, well, I've seen babies do better dribbling,"
he retorted.

"So have I," she said with a grin. "You should see my baby niece, Hope, when she gets going. It's not a pretty sight."

Hunter knew one thing that *was* a pretty sight, and that was Gaylynn, hair tumbling in her eyes, her cheeks flushed, her lips lifted in a smile that softened his heart and hardened other parts of his anatomy.

Damn it, she made another basket, a three-pointer this time.

He managed to pull within one point in their allotted time before the game was over.

Afterward, as he tried to cool down with his head bent and his palms braced on his knees, he was startled to feel her come up from behind him to put her arm around his shoulder and kiss his sweaty cheek. His temperature shot right off the map again.

Straightening, he said, "What was that for?"

"For not being a gentleman and just letting me win. For making me work for it. I won fair and square."

He gave her a surely-you-jest look. "Fair and square? With that outfit on? No way."

"It's not my fault if you get distracted easily," she said with a jaunty grin and a friendly nudge of her shoulder.

"I don't know about you, but I sure could use a cold drink. Come on inside—I've got some soda and beer in the fridge." Taking her acceptance for granted, he moved up the steps. To his surprise, she didn't immediately follow him.

"Is there a problem?" he asked.

There certainly was. Hunter was too damn attractive for his own good. Even sweaty from a basketball game, wearing a simple white T-shirt and jeans. His

hair was damp at the temples, accentuating the streak
of gray there and increasing his wolfish look.

"You've got something against cold drinks?"
Hunter inquired with a lift of a dark eyebrow. "Or are
you afraid that my place will be so messy that you
won't be able to bear it? Come to think of it, maybe
you should wait out here while I go get the drinks. I'm
not exactly a neatnik. Or you can come in and see for
yourself, if you want. The choice is yours."

He went on inside, leaving the front door open.

The choice was hers. She could stand out here and
brood about her increasing attraction to him or she
could go inside and simply enjoy Hunter's company.

Around the edge of the doorway, she saw him prop
open the screen door invitingly. All she could see were
his fingers. The long lean fingers that had soothed a
baby bird's broken wing or caressed Gaylynn's face.
The decision was made. She went inside.

The layout of his cabin was identical to her brother's, with the exception of a large fieldstone fireplace
that took up most of one wall. The place wasn't as
messy as he'd made out, although it did have a definite lived-in look to it. Newspapers were strewn across
the coffee table and a pair of shoes had been left near
the couch, which was brown leather and had a woven
wool blanket on it. On the walls were several paintings
and a mandala. She studied the pieces while watching
Hunter out of the corner of her eye. His home suited
him; it was powerful and elemental. So was he. Very
much so.

Noticing her apparent interest in the paintings, he
said, "The artwork is Cherokee," before asking,
"What can I get you?" as he opened the fridge door.

A new brain, she thought to herself. *The one I've got has a tendency to turn to mush when you're around.*

Aloud she said, "A soda would be fine."

"Do you still eat those awful peanut-butter-and-banana sandwiches?" he asked her as he handed her an icy can.

"You bet. And do you still eat those awful peanut-butter-and-ketchup sandwiches?"

"Absolutely. I'm tempted to make one now..."

"You do and I'm going home," she retorted with a wrinkle of her nose.

They went back out on the shaded front porch to sit in the pair of rockers Hunter had set out there. And as she watched the dappled sunlight strike his craggy face, Gaylynn told herself over and over again: *I will not fall in love with Hunter. I will not fall in love with Hunter. I will not fall in love with Hunter.*

Even as she said the words to herself, she couldn't help wondering if she were trying to close the barn door after the horses were already out.

"Okay, Blue, let's see if the cellular phone works this time," Gaylynn murmured to the kitten as they both sat on the rocker on the front porch.

Michael had given her the phone before she'd left Chicago with instructions to keep in touch. She'd called her parents several times in the past few weeks since she'd arrived. She'd tried to call them even more often but the connection was sketchy. She didn't know why, maybe the surrounding mountains had something to do with it.

"Hi, Papa," Gaylynn greeted her father over the phone, using her nickname for him. "How is everything?"

"Everything is fine here. Hope is taking her first steps and your mother and Brett both used a store full of film while that brother of yours filmed an epic movie of the event."

"And I suppose you sat there unmoved by the momentous event, hmm?" she challenged him teasingly.

"She walks like a little chicken with her elbows stuck out behind her. You looked the same way when you started walking."

They talked for several minutes about Hope before her father said, "Michael tells me that he gave the Rom box to you. Have you opened it yet?"

"Yes."

"And?"

"And nothing."

"Nothing? You saw no one?"

She wasn't about to tell him that she'd seen a derelict-looking old man for fear her protective father would drive right down to get her. "Stop worrying about me, Papa."

"Is Hunter looking out for you?"

"I beat him at basketball today."

"Good for you! All those Bulls games I took you to are paying off now."

"That and the fact that, because of cutbacks at school, I've had to teach gym classes on top of my other work. So I've had lots of practical experience on the basketball court."

"But that was in the past. No more cheap schools. When you come back you'll apply to teach at a good school—St. Basil's, maybe? Along the north shore where all the wealthy kids live."

"Wealthy kids have problems, too," she said.

"So when will you be coming home?" her father asked.

"I'm not sure yet."

"Your mother said I shouldn't pressure you about when you will be returning, but I want you to know that we miss you."

"I know, Papa. I miss you, too. I'll call you again real soon, okay? Bye now." A second later she said, "Oh, wait, I meant to ask you about the medallion inside the Rom box . . ."

But her father had already hung up and the connection went dead. Gaylynn had yet to figure out what all the buttons on the phone did, so she decided to just wait and ask him next time rather than try and use the phone again. Besides, the recharge battery light was flashing red.

Later that evening, it began to rain and a cold wind picked up. Gaylynn went back out on the porch to carry Blue inside, but the kitten didn't trust her enough for that yet. Still, it was too cold for them to stay outside. She couldn't bear to see them shivering.

Putting on her sweatshirt, she kept the front door open, propping open the screen door, as well. Then she tugged on the string that Blue so loved to play with. The kitten pounced on it rambunctiously. To her relief, Spook chased after the string, too, until both kittens were inside the house. It wasn't the first time; they'd meandered inside before but not to stay. This time she quickly shut the door.

More tugging on the string got the kittens into the bedroom. She closed that door and went to get Cleo, stopping first in the kitchen to open a can of cat food, which she used to tempt the mama kitty inside. The

meows of Cleo's two kittens also played a part in the
mother cat deciding to come inside.

Gaylynn had already brought in supplies—cat box
and litter—for the time when she'd be able to cajole the
feline family inside. She quickly let Blue and Spook out
of the bedroom, where they were greeted by their relieved mama. Then all three of them dug into the dishes
of cat food she'd set out, one for each.

After the food was devoured the family of cats proceeded to explore every square inch of the cabin.

"Well, does the place meet with your approval?"
Gaylynn mocking asked them.

Cleo answered with an affirmative "mrrrrow."
Gaylynn already knew that the Siamese was a talkative cat who loved being talked to, and was always well-
bred enough to reply when spoken to. Spook on the
other hand was the silent one and had taken up hiding
under the end table.

But when Gaylynn awoke in the morning it was to
find all three cats on her bed. She'd checked them over
the night before and hadn't found any fleas on them, a
miracle considering the woods surrounding them.
"You're safe now," Gaylynn whispered to a purring
Cleo, whose "prrrrrow" indicated her approval.

Outside, the weather was cold and blustery, with rain
showers that lasted all day long. Wispy froths of mist
would go wafting by, settling over the treetops Gaylynn could see up on the ridge. They were like pieces of
flotsam in a river of clouds, drifting along until they hit
an obstacle, like the ridge, and then sliding along it.
Watching was like looking through a white kaleido-
scope of ever-changing patterns and designs. It was a
great day to stay inside.

The kittens didn't remain in one place long enough for her to sketch them, but Cleo cooperated by curling up on the couch and sleeping there for an hour. Gaylynn was truly impressed by the sketch she did. It actually looked like a cat, and not just any cat but Cleo in particular with the darker markings around her ears and nose.

It wasn't as if Gaylynn was using any fancy art supplies; she'd found a pad of blank paper in her car—a teacher was forever dragging around paper in some shape or form.

But are you still a teacher? an inner voice asked. She did find herself wondering what her kids were doing back in Chicago and feeling that she'd let them down by not being strong enough to see the year out. Several times she'd been tempted to call one of her co-workers at the school and ask how things were going, but something had held her back.

The two kittens provided a welcome diversion as Blue took the phrase "snug as a bug in a rug" literally, diving beneath one of the cotton throw rugs, then turning around and lying down so only her pink nose peeked out. To Gaylynn's surprise a few minutes later, Spook crouched down, playing the unexpected role of "mighty hunter," before pouncing on top of the rug and Blue. In a flash the two kittens were off chasing each other while Gaylynn laughed at their antics.

A knock at the front door around dinnertime sent all the cats diving for cover in the relative safety of her bedroom. "It's just Hunter," she reassured them as she opened the door.

He was standing on her front porch, wearing a gray sweatshirt with a hood. On top of that was an official-looking rain slicker. In his arms were three bags full of food. Not wanting the cats to get out while the door was open, she grabbed his arm and tugged him quickly inside.

"What's all this?" she asked, pointing to the bags.

"Food. My fridge went on the fritz. I hated to see all this food go to waste so I thought I'd store it here."

"You've got enough food there for an army," she noted, peeking over the edge of the paper bag.

"Yeah, well, I'm a growing boy."

"I don't have much in my fridge right now," she admitted, "so you're welcome to store your stuff here."

"Actually, I thought we might as well start eating it, since I don't know when I'll be able to get someone to come out here to look at my fridge."

She eyed him suspiciously. She had a feeling this was his way of looking out for her, of making sure she had enough food in the house, but short of examining his refrigerator there was little she could do, except to cook for him.

So she said, "The least you can do is stay and help me eat some of this food, then."

He needed no convincing.

Gaylynn liked to cook. She found the process soothing. She just wasn't very good at it. So she kept it simple.

Seeing how good Hunter looked with his damp hair tumbling onto his forehead, accentuating the sharp lines of his face, she had a hard time concentrating on her culinary skills.

As she unpacked the food he'd brought, her earlier suspicions returned. "Soup?" she said, holding up one of the half-dozen cans he had in the bag. "Since when do you keep cans of soup in the refrigerator?"

"I had too many cans in the cupboard. They had a sale and I picked up too many... I couldn't even close the door."

Gaylynn wished she could close the door on the provocative thoughts running through her head. Here he was talking about soup and she was eyeing the curve of his lips as he said every word. Aside from the fact that he had to have the sexiest mouth in the northern hemisphere, it occurred to her that she'd never sketched him. And she wanted to. Wanted to keep his likeness beside her for the times when they were apart.

Great. Next, you'll be putting his picture under your pillow, she silently chastised herself, frowning as she seemed to recall that that was part of a Gypsy love spell she'd heard or read about at one time. She didn't need to evoke any more magic; she had enough trouble on her hands as it was.

While she finished preparing two steaks, boiled new potatoes and fresh zucchini, Hunter tried to convince the cats that he wasn't Jack the Ripper. The soft voice he used was enough to make Gaylynn melt.

"You should have Laura check them over to make sure they're all okay," he told Gaylynn as Blue skittishly sniffed his outstretched hand.

"Who is Laura?" Gaylynn asked.

"She's the local vet. She makes house calls in special cases. If I ask her, I'm sure she'd be willing to stop by."

"You know her real well, then?"

His noncommittal "mmm" didn't tell her much at all, and left her feeling as green as the zucchini—green with jealousy.

"She's married," Hunter finally said, his grin making her wonder if he could read her mind.

"That's nice," she managed to say.

"What's this?" Hunter suddenly asked, noticing the engraved metal box on the end table.

"Um, it's a box a relative sent us from Hungary."

"Nice workmanship," he said approvingly.

"Do you notice anything strange about it?" she asked.

"Strange meaning what?"

"It's just that the box has a legend that goes with it. I'll tell you about it some other time."

"Why not now?"

"Because dinner is ready now."

"It looks good," he said.

She could only hope it would taste the same.

Deciding not to test the kitties' table manners, she'd made sure to put out cat food for them in the kitchen so they wouldn't be tempted to jump on the table.

As she sat down, the image of her coaxing the cats inside the evening before suddenly reminded her of the way Hunter had coaxed her to go into his cabin after their basketball game yesterday. Which promptly made her feel like a stray herself.

She wondered if her hair looked all right. She hadn't had time to really look in a mirror since Hunter's unexpected arrival. She still hadn't gotten it cut. And Hunter hadn't gotten his cut, either. It now did more than just brush the collar of his blue shirt; it was at least an inch beyond that. The shaggier his hair got, the sexier he got.

"It's time you got a haircut," she informed him.

"You volunteering for the job?"

"Isn't there a barber in Lonesome Gap?"

"Nope. Mostly the wives cut their husbands' hair. But since I'm not married . . ."

Not falling for his poor-me routine, she asked, "Who cut your hair the last time you had it cut?"

"Some trendy salon over in Summerville."

"Somehow I can't picture you in a trendy salon," Gaylynn replied wryly.

"Thanks. I'll take that as a compliment," he said with a slow smile that lit fires in her heart.

"I, uh . . . Uh, why don't you go back to that salon in Summerville again?"

"They wanted to use mousse on me," he declared with such a look of pure male outrage that Gaylynn cracked up.

"You poor baby," she cooed, patting his arm reassuringly. "Wuz they tryin' to mousse with you?"

He chuckled at her pun before growling, "No one mousses with me!"

At their shared laughter, Gaylynn wondered why it couldn't always be like this between them—free and easy, fun and carefree. Then her eyes caught his and the flashdance of attraction tapped its message into her heartbeat. The want, the need, the yearning, was overwhelming. She checked his expression, wondering if she were the only one feeling these unexpected bursts of passion. His vivid green eyes gave nothing away.

She had to say something, put the conversation on an impersonal level before she let something slip. "Uh, how is your deputy doing? The one who injured his foot?"

"That's a polite way of putting it. He's using a cane to get around and is tied to desk duty for another two weeks."

"Is that why you've been working all those extra hours?"

"So you noticed that, did you?" He seemed pleased.

Now what should she say? That she was as aware of his comings and goings as she was of her own breathing? That she didn't breathe easily at night until she heard the gravel-crunching that heralded the arrival of Hunter's car up the steep driveway. He had to go past her cabin to reach his own. By now, she even recognized the ragged purr of his car's engine.

In the end, Hunter let her off the hook by talking about an emergency call he'd gotten that day, to get Ma Battle's ornery tabby cat out of a tree. "I'm lucky I made it out of there alive," he noted. "Seems that Ma Battle had good ol' Tom neutered and he didn't appreciate the fact one bit."

"Tom being the cat's name, I presume?" Gaylynn inquired.

"That's right."

"Ma Battle is the one who enters all the sweepstakes, isn't she?"

"Right again. Have you met her yet? She hasn't been talking to you, has she?"

"No, I haven't met her yet. Why do you ask if she's been talking to me—is there some law against that?"

"No law against it, no."

"So why did you ask?"

"No reason."

Gaylynn's raised eyebrow told him she wasn't buying that for one minute.

"Okay, I happened to mention that you were a teacher," he admitted reluctantly, "and some folks in town got together and wanted to ask you...something. But I told them not to bother you, that you were here to rest, not to get bogged down with a bunch of kids."

"What on earth are you talking about?"

''Nothing. Don't you even think about it for one minute. You need your rest. You certainly don't need to go traipsing into town and getting involved in their problems.''

''What problems?''

''Nothing. Forget I mentioned it. Great dinner, by the way.''

''Yeah, right. I noticed you gave half of your steak to Blue.''

''I never could resist a pair of gorgeous eyes.''

''I know.'' Which made Gaylynn wish *her* eyes were gorgeous instead of just brown. ''You always did have the heart of a marshmallow,'' she noted in teasing voice.

Hunter just glared at her.

''Why, you're blushing,'' she noted in amazement.

''I am not. Listen, I've got to go. I've got the night shift tonight.'' As he put on his raincoat, he said, ''And remember, don't let anyone drag you into things in town, okay?''

''Will do,'' she said with a cheerful wave, before closing the cabin door.

''Gaylynn will *do* whatever she damn well pleases,'' Hunter muttered under his breath before grinning. ''At least, I *hope* she does!'' That's what he was counting on.

Six

"**Y**ou sure do go through that cat food mighty fast," Floyd noted as Gaylynn plunked four boxes of dried food on the counter. "How many cats you aim on feeding up there?"

"They're growing kitties."

"Yeah, and at the rate they're eating, they'll be growing into ten-foot-high tigers," Floyd said.

Instead of hurrying on her way, as she'd always done before, this time Gaylynn lingered to chat. She had a feeling that there wouldn't be much that happened in Lonesome Gap that Floyd and Bessie didn't know about. And she was curious to know what Hunter had been talking about last night—when he'd said that some folks in town had wanted to ask her something.

But the "something" Floyd and Bessie were talking about now was the semi-truck filled with fertilizer that had tipped over a few weeks before.

"Made a right mess, it did," Bessie noted.

"Not to mention smelling worse than a skunk in heat."

"Now, Floyd Twitty, you mind your manners!" Bessie exclaimed with a wifely bat at his arm.

"This young lady is from Chicago, I'm sure she's heard worse," Floyd retorted. "You're just a worry-wart."

Bessie sniffed. "As I was saying, that accident made a right mess. My cousin Eldon works for the county and was part of the clean-up crew."

"I told Boone he should have gone on down to Summerville and applied for the clean-up job hisself, but he was too busy working on that car of his," Floyd stated.

Seeing Gaylynn's confused look, Bessie said, "Boone is our grandson. His folks died when he was just a tike and we raised him. He's a miracle worker with anything mechanical. He works at the garage attached to our filling station here. Folks bring their cars from all over the county to have Boone work on them."

"I've been telling him he needs to charge them more," Floyd said. "I'm fixing to leave everything to him when we retire, but first I got to see if he has good business sense. Right now all I see is that he's stubborn as a mule."

"He gets that from *your* side of the family," Bessie told her husband.

"Umm, so has anything else been happening in town?" Gaylynn asked, still no closer to figuring out what it was that Hunter had been talking about the night before.

"Well, you no doubt heard about poor Deputy Carberry shooting hisself in the foot like that," Floyd replied.

"It was so embarrassing," Bessie added.

"Not to mention painful," Floyd tacked on.

"I meant for his wife," Bessie elaborated. "Here she'd been putting on airs and bragging on about how Lonesome Gap was lucky to have a lawman like Charlie Carberry."

"And we are. Ain't many lawmen know how to shoot themselves in the foot like that!" Floyd said with a cackle and a slap to his knee.

"Now, Floyd, it ain't seemly to be laughing at others' misfortunes," Bessie said as she bit back the laughter herself. "Is there anything else we can help you with, honey?" she asked Gaylynn.

"I guess not. Oh, wait. You could recommend a good place to eat lunch in town." Gaylynn was getting tired of her own cooking, such as it was, and decided that while she was doing a little research and reconnaissance, she might as well grab some food while she was at it.

"Why, sure," Bessie replied. "You just mosey on down to the Lonesome Café and get some of the best milk-breaded catfish you ever did taste."

"The café is right next door to Hazel's Hash House," Floyd added. "Well, actually, it's in the same building, if you want to get technical about it."

"Which I don't," Bessie stated. "There's no need to get into the details of the feud between the Montgomeries and the Rues, and why Hazel Rue set up her hash house in the same building as dear Lillie Montgomery. This town would have been much better off if those trouble-making Rues had stayed over in their own hollow 'stead of coming to town.''

Unable to stand the suspense a moment longer, Gaylynn asked, ''Does this feud have something to do with a question the town wanted to ask me?''

''Why, no,'' Bessie said in surprise. ''But we're not allowed to talk about that. Goodness gracious, Hunter would skin me alive if I said anything to you about . . . the other matter,'' she ended in a confidential undertone.

''What 'other matter'?'' Gaylynn asked.

''I really can't say. Now don't you worry none. I didn't mean to scare you with all this talk of feuding.''

''What caused the feud?''

''I don't rightly know.''

''I do,'' Floyd interjected. ''Caleb Montgomery turned his neighbor, Paul Rue, in to the revenue men and the Rues . . . well, they had a nasty way of getting even.''

''By revenue men, you mean the Internal Revenue Service?'' Gaylynn said. ''This was a tax matter?''

''It was more of a *moonshine* matter,'' Floyd replied.

''How long ago did this feud start?''

''I believe it was in 1927.''

''That's almost fifty years ago.''

''Just a blink of an eye in these mountains' time clock,'' Floyd maintained.

''Do any Montgomeries or Rues live up near my brother's cabin?'' Gaylynn asked.

''No. What makes you ask?''

''It's just that I saw an elderly man up near the woods, and he looked rather, um, disreputable.''

"That description would fit half the men in this town," Bessie interjected.

Gaylynn didn't know what the protocol was in matters of this nature. Were moonshiners still around? Should she just come right out and ask if there were any stills up there? Even if she did, she doubted she'd get an honest answer. Friendly as Bessie and Floyd were, Gaylynn was still an outsider here. For the time being.

Not wondering what that mental amendment meant, she decided now was as good a time as any to head over to the café for some lunch. "Well, I'd better get going. Thanks for filling me in about the town feud."

"Yep, Lonesome Gap has its very own feud," Floyd bragged, "just like in that Shakespeare movie we rented on video, with the Montagues and Capillaries."

"Capulets," Gaylynn automatically corrected him.

"Caplets? No, we don't sell any of that stuff here, but they might have some over at the café. They sell headache pills there along with those fizzie stomach caplets. Don't know why. The cooking is good. Eating there never did give me any trouble, not that I can say the same for the wife's cooking," Floyd stated.

"Just for that, I'm making liver and onions tonight," Bessie announced.

Floyd rolled his eyes and made a grimace that made his wrinkled face look even more like a basset hound.

Gaylynn left them to their marital sparring. Going outside, she paused long enough to bend down and pet Bo Regard—whereupon he lifted his head and actually moved one ear, as well. "Don't strain yourself," Gaylynn murmured teasingly.

The bloodhound responded by dropping his head back to the doormat he all but covered.

Lonesome Gap was small enough that Gaylynn could walk from one end to the next without much trouble. The day was clear and sunny, the mountains providing a verdant backdrop. She didn't know which view she preferred most, the one from here in the narrow valley looking up, or the one from the top of the mountains looking across at the layer after layer of blue ridges that gave this area its name.

Situated as it was between the river and the highway, the town of Lonesome Gap was spread out like the beads on a necklace. Not that there were many beads on this particular necklace; there were less than three dozen buildings in all and half of those were homes. The others were a real estate/video store, several empty storefronts for lease, the Blue Moon Motel with four "cottages with color TV," something called the Gallery of Gifts and a big roadside sign for the Laughing Horse stables in nearby Summerville.

From the front of the building housing both Hazel's Hash House and the Lonesome Café, Gaylynn could see across the road where two churches rested along the lowest hill, as did a small schoolhouse. It seemed as if even more foliage was blooming down here than up on the ridge where her brother's cabin was located. The azalea bushes in front of several houses were loaded with fiery red or pale purple blossoms.

In between buildings were green sections of open land. The sheriff's office was at the far end of town. Gaylynn could see it through the café window at the table she'd chosen before a gum-chewing waitress with big hair in a bold red color greeted her with a smile. The café was busy but not overly so.

"Howdy, I'm Darlene, your waitress." She handed Gaylynn a plastic-coated menu. "Would you like some coffee? No? Well, then I'll be with you in a jiffy."

Gaylynn ended up ordering the catfish and a glass of iced tea. As she waited for her food to arrive, she found herself absently sketching on one of the café's paper napkins. Her subject was the abandoned barn located just beyond the sheriff's office. The building was leaning at a forty-five-degree angle and the afternoon sunlight shone on the weathered wood, turning it a silvery gray.

"Hey, you're mighty good at that," Darlene noted as she plunked down a plate filled with food in front of her, careful not to hit the napkin sketch. "Are you an artist or something?"

"Not really. The way the sunlight was hitting the barn, it just inspired me, I guess."

"That barn has done plenty of inspiring. Used to be a lovers' meeting place, or so I'm told. That was before my time. Then the walls started leaning too bad."

"That place has been leaning like that since Eisenhower was president," a second, older waitress noted as she passed by.

"And the pool has been going almost that long, too," a man at the next table said.

"You gotta learn to develop patience if you live in Lonesome Gap," his tablemate declared. Both men looked as old as the hills.

"You down here on vacation?" the talkative Darlene asked Gaylynn.

"Something like that."

"Where are you headed to?"

"Actually, I'm staying right here in Lonesome Gap. My brother has a cabin not too far from Hunter's."

"You a friend of Hunter?" the man at the other table asked.

"Oh, Hunter and I go way back," Gaylynn replied. "We practically grew up together."

"Well, I'll be a monkey's uncle. Don't that beat all," the man said. "You're not from these parts, though."

"I'm from Chicago."

"I remember now. Hunter's folks up and moved north for some period of time. Then the cold got too much and they ended up retiring to Florida."

"Say, has anyone invited you to join us in the town pool?" his lunchmate asked her.

"I didn't know Lonesome Gap had a pool," Gaylynn said.

"Sure we do."

"It's still a little chilly for swimming, though," she noted.

"Who said anything about swimming? The town is taking bets as to when that doggone barn will actually fall down, which is why no one wants to knock it down."

"I thought you were talking about a swimming pool."

"What would we be needing with a swimming pool when we got inner tubes and the Bitty River? The two were made for each other. There's nothing sweeter than lazing a hot summer day away lying in an inner tube in the river, just letting the world pass you by."

"The world always passes by this town," one of the few younger residents complained from the lunch counter.

"Now don't you go bellyaching, Boone Twitty," Darlene teasingly reprimanded him.

Gaylynn looked for, and sure enough found, the family resemblance between Boone and his grandparents. The young man had the same piercing light blue eyes but not the wrinkles.

"This town is so small it says Welcome To Lonesome Gap on both sides of the sign," Boone stated.

"At least we've *got* a welcome sign," Darlene retorted.

"Only because the Ladies Auxiliary League painted it on an old board one day," Boone said.

"That's not all the Ladies Auxiliary does," a woman with bluish silver hair said from the corner table. She had an accent thicker than molasses. "Why, we have quilting bees, too. Made that bear-paw design quilt you see hanging on the wall over yonder. And we do some dabbling in other things, as well. My name is Gladys Battle but everyone 'round here calls me Ma Battle," she told Gaylynn with a wide smile.

"She's gonna win one of those million-dollar sweepstakes one of these days, right, Ma Battle?" Boone teased her.

"Darn right. Now stop your interrupting so the poor girl can introduce herself."

"I'm Gaylynn Janos."

"Say, you aren't the teacher, are you?" one of the older men at the table across from her suddenly asked.

"I was a teacher up in Chicago, yes. Why do you ask?"

Before the man could answer, the door opened and Hunter strolled into the café. Sizing up the situation, he said, "Now what are you folks telling Gaylynn here?"

"We didn't tell her about the library being closed for five years now and our kids not having anyplace to go what with the cutbacks at school and their library there being so small, not to mention miles away," Darlene stated with several snaps of her gum.

"You just told her," Hunter declared with a frown.

"Did not," the waitress denied.

"Sure you did."

"I told *you,* Hunter," Darlene maintained. "Ain't my fault if'n she heard."

"Why has the library been closed for five years?" Gaylynn inserted.

"Because our last librarian ran off with a no-account lounge lizard," one of the men at the table next to her replied.

"That's not true," Darlene protested. "You're just jealous 'cause she wouldn't go out with you, Orville. Truth is Miz Russell retired. The woman was seventy if she was a day."

"Doesn't change the fact that she ran off with that karaoke singer from the VFW Hall over in Summerville," Orville declared.

"You couldn't hire anyone else to replace her?" Gaylynn asked.

"Actually, we never did *hire* her," Darlene said.

"She worked for free," Boone inserted.

"Only because her aunt was once-removed from the former mayor's first cousin. So she felt it was her duty, after she retired from working up in Chattanooga, to come back home and hold up the family tradition of serving the public."

"None of this is your problem, Gaylynn," Hunter told her as he joined her and tried to distract her by waving a dessert menu. "They have the best apple cobbler here. Want some?"

But Gaylynn was having none of it. "Tell me more about this library," she told Darlene.

"We could show it to you—it's not more than a stone's throw from here," Darlene said.

"Now, Darlene, Gaylynn has better things to do than go exploring some old ramshackle building. You go on now, and let her eat in peace."

"Ignore him," Gaylynn told the waitress.

"Can't do that, hon. He's the law hereabouts." With a saucy grin and another snap of her gum, Darlene added, "I'll just go see if there's any apple cobbler left."

"Be sure you save me a piece," Hunter called after her.

"You think you're so cute," Gaylynn began when Hunter cut her off by stealing a handful of French fries from her plate.

"As I recall, you're the one who thought I was cute," Hunter drawled before biting a fry in half.

She watched the movement of his square jaw as he chewed, noting that it was just as stubbornly gorgeous as ever.

"You're staring, Red."

"Don't call me that," she said with an irritable glare in his direction. "And get your hands off my fries!"

Hunter was tempted to touch *more* than her fries. She was wearing a red T-shirt with lace around a scooped neckline. It was dainty looking and gave him just enough of a peek at her cleavage that he wanted to see more.

He paused with a fry in midair as his gaze became fixed on the curve of her breasts. She was breathing fast, judging from their rapid rise and fall. He'd always thought of her as a little bitty thing, but there was nothing little or bitty about her breasts. His hands itched to hold her, to run his thumbs over the rosy crests, to cradle their lushness in his palms.

That kiss they'd shared in the woods the other day had kept him up nights, literally. Cold showers at 2:00 a.m. were no laughing matter. So what was it about Gaylynn that had him so hot and bothered? Was it the sexy fullness of her lower lip or the fire in her brown eyes? What was happening to him?

Hunter had no idea how long he would have stayed in that sudden trance had it not been for Gaylynn suddenly leaning forward and biting into the fry he still held suspended in midair.

The brush of her lips against his fingertips sent a coil of hunger through him. Her look of triumph left him speechless. Or had his capacity to speak been stolen by the siren pitch of her laughter? Either way, the fierceness of his attraction to her struck him dumb.

As if aware that something was going on, Gaylynn gave Hunter a questioning look.

Their eyes caught hold and remained locked. The noise in the café faded into insignificance. The look in his eyes was a potent visual caress and had a disturbing effect on her metabolism. Time stopped; she didn't know if two seconds or two minutes went by. She only knew that she'd never seen anything as fascinating— the subtle change of Hunter's expression, the way the sunlight coming in through the café window glanced off his eyelashes, the laugh lines at the outer edge of his eyes, the responsiveness . . .

"Here you go, two apple cobblers, fresh as they come," Darlene appeared out of nowhere to announce.

Startled out of their reverie, Hunter and Gaylynn both started in surprise, nearly upsetting the two bowls that Darlene was in the process of setting on the table for them.

"Lordy, you two are as jumpy as a pair of grasshoppers on a hot sidewalk," the waitress noted with a laugh and a snap of her gum before hurrying off to give an impatient Boone his check.

Gaylynn longed for something brilliant to say, but her mind was mush. So instead, she grabbed a spoon and started eating. The apple cobbler was indeed delicious. The combination of the tartness of the apple, the flakiness of the crust and the chill of the vanilla ice cream on top created a tantalizing treat.

Also tantalizing was the memory of the look Hunter had just given her. She'd never seen him looking at her quite that way before. As if he were feeling some of the things she was, as if the magnetic pull was affecting him as it was her.

Or was it just wishful thinking?

"So which of these two wreaths do you like better? The one with the lilac ribbon and the teddy bear or the rose ribbon and the flowers?" Gaylynn asked Hunter. He'd insisted on accompanying her around Lonesome Gap for the remainder of his lunch hour. With him at her side, she wasn't able to get any more information about the library.

She thought the fastest way to send him on his way was to take him shopping at the Gallery of Gifts, the only gift store in town. It hadn't worked. Actually, the store was more a gallery of individual booths from a dozen or so crafts people in the area. On display and for sale was everything from wooden bowls and floral

THE EDITOR'S "THANK YOU" FREE GIFTS INCLUDE:

▶ Four BRAND-NEW romance novels
▶ A Cuddly Teddy Bear

PLACE
FREE GIFT
SEAL
HERE

YES! I have placed my Editor's "thank you" seal in the space provided above. Please send me 4 free books and a Cuddly Teddy Bear. I understand I am under no obligation to purchase any books, as explained on the back and on the opposite page.

225 CIS A4UC (U-SIL-D-10/96)

NAME

ADDRESS   APT.

CITY   STATE   ZIP

Thank you!

DETACH AND MAIL CARD TODAY!

THE SILHOUETTE READER SERVICE™: HERE'S HOW IT WORKS

Accepting free books places you under no obligation to buy anything. You may keep the books and gift and return the shipping statement marked "cancel". If you do not cancel, about a month later we will send you 6 additional novels, and bill you just $2.90 each plus 25¢ delivery and applicable sales tax, if any*. That's the complete price, and—compared to cover prices of $3.50 each—quite a bargain! You may cancel at any time, but if you choose to continue, every month we'll send you 6 more books, which you may either purchase at the discount price…or return to us and cancel your subscription.

*Terms and prices subject to change without notice. Sales tax applicable in N.Y.

If offer card is missing write to: Silhouette Reader Service, 3010 Walden Ave., P.O. Box 1867, Buffalo, NY 14240-1867

BUSINESS REPLY MAIL

FIRST-CLASS MAIL   PERMIT NO. 717   BUFFALO, NY

POSTAGE WILL BE PAID BY ADDRESSEE

SILHOUETTE READER SERVICE
3010 WALDEN AVE
PO BOX 1867
BUFFALO, NY 14240-9952

NO POSTAGE
NECESSARY
IF MAILED
IN THE
UNITED STATES

wreaths to matted photographs of the mountains and exquisite handmade quilts.

Gaylynn hadn't been "shopping" in weeks. She used to enjoy it, before the attack. The place was empty aside from herself, Hunter and the proprietress who turned out to be none other than Ma Battle herself.

"I like to keep busy," she said. "Hunter, I haven't seen you in here in a month of Sundays."

"I'm just giving Gaylynn the grand tour."

"So you'll be taking her over to the library building, too, then?"

"No, ma'am," he replied.

"I just love it when he gets all respectful," Ma Battle told Gaylynn with a grin. "Reminds me of the days when I was his Sunday school teacher and I used to catch him putting chewing gum in the girls' hair."

"He hadn't grown out of that when he moved up to Chicago," Gaylynn told the older woman. "He put chewing gum in my hair once. Only once, though."

"Her father told me he'd put a nasty Gypsy curse on me if I ever tried something like that again," Hunter said. "I never did."

"I guess I was just too soft on him," Ma Battle said. "Despite my name, I really am—"

"A marshmallow," Hunter completed for her. "I've been accused of the same thing myself."

"My, no, you're not a marshmallow. You're much more like a wolf with a gleam in your eye and a heart of gold," Ma Battle declared.

"I'll second that appraisal," Gaylynn agreed.

"You're the one who said I was a marshmallow," he reminded her.

"I was wrong. Ma Battle's description is much more accurate. Now to get back to this wreath, which one do you think is cuter?"

"What makes you think I'm an expert on cute?"

"You're absolutely right. Ma Battle, which one do *you* like better?"

"What is the color scheme of the room where you want to put the wreath?" she asked with feminine practicality.

"Good point. It's for the living room, which has no color scheme at the moment. The couch is a leftover relic in gold and avocado green. But I plan on recovering it in a blue-and-white gingham."

"Rose goes very nicely with blue," Ma Battle suggested.

"You're right. But I like the purple one, too. I guess I'll just get both," she decided. "With a white chenille bedspread, I could make the color scheme in the bedroom white and purple."

"Michael will just love that," Hunter muttered.

"What he doesn't see won't hurt him," Gaylynn countered. "And I'll take that large blue-and-white ceramic bowl with Popcorn painted on the bottom of it, too. It'll look great on the dining room table."

"It's almost as *big* as the dining room table," Hunter stated mockingly. To Ma Battle he said, "So how's ol' Tom doing today? Has he recovered from his tree-climbing expedition yesterday?"

"I don't rightly believe that ol' Tom actually knows he's a cat," the older woman answered. "He chases flies instead of playing with his cat toys. And he's afraid of heights, which is why poor Hunter here had to come rescue him from that tree. He is a dear boy, though."

"Hunter or Tom?" Gaylynn asked with a grin.

"Both of them," Ma Battle replied in kind. "I must admit that I'm particularly partial to cats. How about yourself?"

"She's already taken in a family of three cats," Hunter answered on Gaylynn's behalf.

"A mama cat and her two kittens," Gaylynn went on to elaborate. "She's a Siamese, and her one kitten, Blue, is a cream-colored Siamese. The second kitten, Spook, is a calico."

"Really? How unusual," Ma Battle said. "I can't imagine what the daddy must have been like."

"You sure it wasn't Tom?" Hunter asked her. "In his rowdier days?"

Ma Battle slapped his arm. "Now don't you go saying things like that about my ol' Tom. Where did you find those kittens, up by your cabin?"

Gaylynn nodded.

"That's clear on the other side of the river, too far for Tom to wander," the older woman stated.

"I don't know," Hunter murmured with a wicked grin. "When a man feels the urge he's likely to travel as far as it takes."

"You're speaking from personal experience, of course," Gaylynn inquired tartly, wondering how many women Hunter had "traveled" for while knowing damn well there hadn't been *any* men she'd "traveled" for.

"A gentleman never discusses such matters," he drawled.

"Yeah, right," Gaylynn muttered.

"You done shopping now?" Ma Battle asked her.

"Yeah, I guess I am," Gaylynn replied.

Gaylynn and Hunter walked out of the store with an armload of purchases, his arms filled even more than hers as he insisted on carrying her things back to her car for her. She'd left her trusty American-made subcompact back at the Pit Stop with the Twittys' approval. The car's red color was no longer showroom bright, and the doors showed nicks and dings that came from having to park it on the streets of Chicago for the past five years, but it was still her baby, having given her many seasons of dependable service.

So why was it that the car looked so much smaller when Hunter stood beside it? And it *felt* so much smaller when she and Hunter kept bumping shoulders as they loaded the back seat and trunk with her purchases.

"Thanks for the help," she muttered, almost catching his hand in the trunk in her hurry to close it and get on her way. She wasn't having a panic attack like she'd gotten when she'd been back in Chicago. No, this case of nerves was completely hormone-driven and Hunter-caused. Gaylynn likened it to staring at a box of imported Belgian chocolates for too long without being able to bite into one. She'd been in close proximity with Hunter for the past hour—long enough to want to take a long leisurely nibble.

She had to leave before she said or did something stupid! "Thanks for your help. See you—"

"I could use a lift back to the sheriff's office," he interrupted her.

"It's not that far," she replied. "You can't walk it?"

"Carrying all those packages of yours plumb wore me out."

"Right. And if I believe that, you've got some great swampland to sell me, right?"

"Well, if it's that inconvenient for you..." he began with such a hangdog expression that she had to smile, albeit reluctantly.

"You look like Bo Regard over there."

"Flattery will get you nowhere," Hunter said.

"Come on, I'll give you a lift."

In her eagerness to avoid further exposure to temptation, Gaylynn would have exceeded the posted speed limits just a smidgen were it not for the fact that she had a police officer in her passenger seat. As it was, the drive took a lengthy five minutes.

"Here you are," she noted with false cheerfulness. "Door-to-door chauffeur service."

Instead of getting out, Hunter said, "While you're here why don't you come on in and meet my deputy. His feelings will be hurt if you don't."

Her hopes of a fast getaway were fading fast. Besides, she still hadn't had the opportunity to check out the abandoned library building. And the more Hunter tried to keep her away from it, the more determined she was to find it. Perhaps not today, but soon.

Hunter's deputy, Charlie Carberry, turned out to be a squeaky-clean-cut, very polite young man with a nervously bobbing Adam's apple who was actually more interested in going on his lunch hour than passing the time of day with her. "Nice to meet you," he said with a tip of his cap. "I'll be going to lunch now, Hunter. It's my day for Hazel's Hash House."

"What did he mean by that?" Gaylynn asked after Charlie left.

"We alternate between the two restaurants. That way no one's feelings get hurt."

"You mean because of the feud between the Rues and the Montgomeries?"

"Ah, you heard about that, did you?"

She nodded.

Instead of going into more detail about it, he changed the subject. "So what do you think of my stomping grounds?"

"Tack a few girlie posters on the wall and it would look just like your old tree house."

Hunter grinned at her tart comment. This was the Gaylynn he knew and loved. Whoa there, he ordered his runaway thoughts. Love? Where had that come from? Is that what was wrong with him? No way! Falling for Gaylynn would be like eating gunpowder—you know it's going to detonate. And he knew Gaylynn was going back to her life in Chicago sooner or later. Both scenarios were liable to leave him hurting if he was foolish enough to expose himself to harm.

But damn, she looked good in those jeans.

"So are you going to show me your weapons?" she inquired mockingly. "Or is that only with the more expensive tour?"

He imagined her touring his body with those supple fingers of hers, fingers devoid of rings or nail polish.

Seeing the dazed look in his eyes, she said, "Yo, Hunter, are you feeling okay?"

"Absolutely," he said with only slightly less than his usual certainty. "Want to see my extra-heavy-duty handcuffs?" He tugged open the top drawer and dangled them in front of her.

"Can I use 'em on you?" she inquired.

Not trusting that fiendish gleam in her eye one bit—was it caused by passion or anticipation of getting even with him for that gum in her hair all those years ago?—he heard himself saying, "Only if we're in bed."

Her eyes widened. Did he really mean that? Or was he just pulling her leg? That naughty grin made it hard for her to tell.

Looking away, she asked, "So where are your 'wanted' pictures?"

"Bessie has some over near the post-office corner."

"She said she has to keep Floyd from drawing mustaches on them."

"He has an unusual sense of humor," Hunter acknowledged.

"Like someone else I know," Gaylynn muttered. "You're not doing a very good job as a tour guide, you know."

"Sorry." He dropped the cuffs back in the top desk drawer and closed it. "There's not all that much to see, actually. This is the office, pretty standard. Two desks, phones, one fax machine, filing cabinets and the rest of your regulation office equipment. We have one holding cell in the back—" He opened a door to show it to her. "That door over there leads to the john. The radio room is here—it's more like a radio *closet* actually. And that's about it."

Gaylynn had gotten progressively quieter as the tour progressed. Seeing him in such official surroundings brought home the fact that he was a man who carried a gun for a living.

"Something wrong?" he asked her.

Gaylynn shook her head, reminding herself that Lonesome Gap wasn't Chicago and Hunter wasn't exposed to the dangers here that he was up there. But still, all it took was one crazed person . . .

She closed her eyes and gathered her composure.

"So are you aiming on heading straight on back to the cabin now?" he asked her.

Opening her eyes, she nodded.

"Maybe I'll see you later on, then," he said, brushing his fingers down her cheek.

She wondered if he'd done that just to distract her. If so, it worked.

Gaylynn had actually given up her plans for scouting out the old library building that afternoon, but when circumstances unfolded in such a way that she got the opportunity, she took it. With both hands.

She passed the turnoff to the library on her way home. The sign was rusty and almost illegible, but she saw it. And she took the turn.

The brick building was locked. Weeds grew along the steps leading to the front door. Was the place empty or was it still full of books? Noticing the high-set windows along the side wall, Gaylynn couldn't resist taking a peek. Which meant pulling herself up to peer in the dirt-smeared windows. It took her three tries before she succeeded at what amounted to doing a chin-up a foot off the grassy ground. She had one foot wedged against the basement window frame for leverage.

She'd just gotten high enough to get a quick look when she suddenly felt a pair of broad male hands span her waist. Before she could scream, Hunter drawled, "And what do you think you're doing?"

Seven

"Me?" Gaylynn shrieked in anger. "What do you think *you're* doing?" she demanded as he easily held her with her feet dangling a few inches off the ground.

"Looks like I'm catching a trespasser," Hunter replied.

She tried to wiggle out of his grasp, but her movements only served to increase the intimacy of their embrace. Her fanny was inadvertently rubbing against the placket of his pants.

"Are you resisting arrest, ma'am?" he asked in a husky whisper.

She was trying to resist the excitement shooting through her system. He'd parted his legs to brace himself, so there was no mistaking the way his body was responding to hers. She could feel his taut arousal burning through the back of her jeans. Just when she thought her heart would leap from her breast, he put her down, only to turn her in his arms so that they were now face-to-face.

"You're in a heap of trouble," he whispered.

"I can tell," she whispered in return.

Gaylynn couldn't help herself. She had the strongest urge to kiss him. So she did.

The moment had been building since they'd shared that long heated look at the café, the one that could melt steel.

At first her lips merely brushed his with playful intent. He allowed her to tease him this way for several seconds before deepening the pressure of his mouth against hers with a gentle charm that drove her lips apart and allowed him entrance.

Instead of pressing his advantage immediately, he paused to tantalize the corner of her mouth with a string of kisses. Then he focused erotic sips, teasing nips and sweet swirls of his tongue on the lushness of her lower lip.

By now Gaylynn was trembling in her shoes, not from fear but from need. She *needed* to have him kiss her, not merely sample her as if she were a fine wine. She was all set to speak her thoughts when Hunter interpreted them on his own, homing in on her mouth and devouring it with a darkly erotic kiss of infinite duration.

His mouth slanted against hers with hungry impatience as he threaded his fingers through her silky hair to cup the back of her head, bracing her against the reverent intrusion of his probing tongue.

Gaylynn slid her arms around his waist and leaned into the kiss, depending on him as much as her own two legs to hold her upright. The circle of his arms grew smaller as he molded her more tightly against him.

One of his hands remained entangled in her hair while the other slid down her back to cup her bottom and tug her against him—so that not even the spring breeze fit between them.

She wanted him with a hunger and desperation that shocked her...made her forget where she was, who she was. All she cared about was kissing him, being kissed by him, exploring the contours of his body, learning what pleased him. She could feel his reaction when she tickled the roof of his mouth with her tongue. He liked that. So did she.

One kiss blended directly into the next with a fluid interplay that left her trembling. He sipped at her mouth. Then he slanted his parted lips over hers, his tongue stroking hers familiarly, boldly, intimately.

His hands were as busy as his mouth, always moving, surveying her feminine curves with silent appreciation. When he tugged her red T-shirt from the waistband of her jeans, she sighed in anticipation. Teasing her, he let several seconds elapse before sliding his hand beneath the knit cotton material to rest against her bare skin. She shivered with delight.

Finally! *Finally* he was touching her, bare skin to bare skin, his fingertips leisurely strolling up her back. She wanted to hurry him along. So she tried to tug his shirt from the belted waistband of his slacks. Nothing happened. His shirt remained where it was.

She got distracted by the fact that he was kissing his way from her mouth to the curve of her ear. The warm moistness of his breath nearly undid her. So did the curve of his hand as he stole beneath her arm to brush the side of her breast. The silky material of her bra did more to amplify his touch than to protect her from it.

Not that she wanted protecting. She didn't. She wanted to explore him the way he was exploring her. She lowered her hands from his shoulders to his chest, but she longed to feel the warmth of his bare skin instead of the warmth of his shirt.

Buttons. Her fingers went in search of them. She managed to get two undone before *she* came undone as he nibbled her earlobe, gently blowing and then swirling his tongue along the shell-like curve. A simple caress to enflame such pleasure. In all her twenty-nine years, no one had ever kissed her like that before. This was a first she shared with Hunter.

She wanted to share more. Excitement burned within her. The muffled sound of a "wuff" barely registered on the frayed edges of her composure. But the feel of a wet nose pressed against the small of her bare back was enough to make her gasp in surprise and break off their heated embrace.

"Wha...at?" Gaylynn barely recognized the bloodhound in an upright position. She'd only seen him horizontal. "I've never seen Bo Regard up before," she said in surprise.

"He's not the only one who's *up*," Hunter muttered, drawing in a ragged breath. To the dog he said, "Go away, Bo."

The bloodhound replied with a woof and sat back on its haunches, about a foot away from them.

"What are you doing out here?" Gaylynn asked.

"Are you talking to me or to the dog?" Hunter retorted.

"Both of you."

"Well, I can't speak for Bo Regard," he said solemnly, "but I'm here to keep you out of trouble."

Instead of responding to his claim, she asked, "Who has the keys to the padlock on the library door?"

"Well, I do, but—"

"That's great! Then you can open the building up while you're here and I can take a look inside."

"Now, Gaylynn, you don't want to go getting involved in this," he said.

"Yes, I do," she interrupted him. "Come on, open it up."

"Okay." He opened his mouth as if he were at the dentist, sticking his tongue out at her and wiggling it for extra measure.

"Very funny! You know I meant the library building."

It was all Hunter could do to hide a huge smile. His plan was working!

Careful to keep an outwardly disapproving look on his face, he moved toward the padlocked front door with marked reluctance. "I don't know about this…"

"Well, I do," she stated firmly. "Come on, hurry up and unlock it."

"The place was been boarded up for five years, Gaylynn. It's not going anywhere."

But *she* would be going somewhere, he thought to himself. Going back to her city home. Already there was a change in her, a newfound purpose. Which was as it should be. That was what he wanted, right? Despite the kisses they'd just shared, kisses powerful enough to practically melt his regulation shoes.

His brooding gaze settled on Gaylynn once more. She was standing beneath the carved wooden sign that said Lonesome Gap Lending Library. Seeing her curious look at it, Hunter said, "Floyd made that. Back in the forties, I think. He used to do a lot of woodcarving before his eyes went bad on him."

When he finally removed the padlock and opened the creaky door, Gaylynn hurried to move past him, but he held her arm. "Watch out for snakes. Not to mention mice and spiders."

"All of which I've had in my classroom at one time or another as part of some natural science project."

"Running loose?"

"At times," she acknowledged with a rueful smile.

Actually, Hunter had already checked the place out the day before, but he didn't want her knowing that.

Gaylynn's attention was focused on the inside of the building, which naturally was dusty—but that was to be expected. Cobwebs hung from the ceilings, like those decorating the haunted house that was set up at her neighborhood church every Halloween. Only these suckers were the real thing.

Reminding herself that she'd once had a daddy longlegs as a pet, she moved forward.

The place looked as if it had been hastily closed. Chairs were still pulled out around a wooden table. A clock on the wall was stuck at three minutes after three. Layers of dust covered everything. White sheets, now turned gray, had been tossed over most of the bookcases, which were for the most part empty of books.

A loud sneeze had her saying, "Gesundheit" before she realized that it was Bo Regard who'd sneezed. He was laying on the threshold and, with the exuberance of his sneeze, somehow one of his long ears had ended up clear over on the other side of his head. The dog looked so startled that Gaylynn had to laugh.

Hunter almost kissed her again there and then. *Seducing her isn't part of the plan,* he firmly reminded himself.

Aloud he said, "Seen enough?"

"Where are all the books?"

"I believe they were put in the safe keeping of the Ladies Auxiliary League. You'd have to check with Ma Battle."

"I aim to," Gaylynn replied just like a native.

Hunter could already see her making plans for the place. "You didn't come down here to the mountains to work," he reminded her.

"Don't worry about me," she said with an absent pat to his cheek. "You go on back to the sheriff's office and I'll lock up."

Wiping the dusty smudge she'd inadvertently left on his cheek, Hunter couldn't stop his grin from showing this time. "I'll leave Bo Regard here to keep you company."

"That's nice."

"The two of you don't do any pirouettes up on the rooftop now, y'hear," he drawled, knowing darn well that Gaylynn wasn't listening to a word he said.

"We won't," she murmured.

Hooking an arm around her waist, Hunter tugged her to him and planted a smacking kiss on her startled lips. "Welcome back," he whispered, running his fingertips down her cheek. A second later he was gone.

"That man is going to drive me to distraction," Gaylynn told Bo Regard.

"I heard that," Hunter called from outside.

"Good," she shouted back. "I meant you to!"

Satisfied that she'd gotten in the last word, she focused her attention on listing what had to be done to get the library open again, even if on a limited basis. It felt good to have a project to focus on again.

"I thought that was your car I saw over here," Bessie Twitty noted from the doorway. "I left Floyd minding the store while I moseyed over here to see what was what. Hello there, Bo Regard. You getting curious in your old age?"

"Is he a very old dog?" Gaylynn asked. "Is that why he's so...sedentary?"

"Is that a dog disease or something?" Bessie asked suspiciously.

"No, the term can apply to people, too."

"Well, to answer your question, no one rightly knows how old Bo Regard is, but it's somewhere around four years or so. He just is picky about where he goes visiting. If'n he likes a place, he just plunks hisself down and stays there for a long spell. Not a bad life, if you ask me."

"You're absolutely right."

"So what do you think of the lending library? The place has gotten kinda rundown over the years."

"I can see that. Tell me more about the library," Gaylynn requested. "Who do you think could benefit most by its being reopened again?"

"Why, the children, of course. They used it before and I'm sure they would use it again. The little ones used to sit around on the floor while Miz Russell would sit in that big rocking chair over there in the corner and read to them from a fancy picture book."

"Hunter said that the Ladies Auxiliary League is storing the books."

"That's right. I'm a member, so is Ma Battle. There are a dozen or so of us, mostly from right here in

Lonesome Gap, but some from a bit farther out, from the small farms scattered around.''

"Would the Ladies Auxiliary League be interested in helping me clean the place up?"

"I suppose so. What for?"

"To reopen the library."

"With you as the librarian? Why, that's a wonderful idea!" Bessie exclaimed, giving Gaylynn an exuberant hug. "So things worked out just as Hunter wanted, after all."

"What do you mean?"

"Nothing," Bessie hurriedly said. "My mouth runs away from me sometimes and I don't know what I'm saying."

"Wait a minute! Are you saying that Hunter wanted me to be the librarian here? That he wanted me to reopen the library?"

"We wanted the library reopened, but none of us knows the first thing about libraries. Now organizing a quilting bee or something of that nature is another matter. We do have our specialties, but libraries..." Bessie shook her head. "That's not one of them."

"Let's get back to Hunter for a minute," Gaylynn said. "What did you mean ... ?"

"Oh my, that sounded like Floyd a'calling me. I'd best be going."

"I didn't hear anything."

"A wife always knows when her husband is a'calling for her. I'm so glad you'll be reopening the library and I'll get the Ladies Auxiliary gathered up any time you want. You just let me know."

"I'll let you know all right. A woman always knows when her husband is a'calling. In a pig's ear! A woman always knows when she's been had," Gaylynn muttered after Bessie hurried out. Looking back on Hunter's actions during the past twenty-four hours, she could see a definite pattern. Dropping hints about her being needed in town, telling her not to get involved.

"Why, that so-and-so!" she said so loud that Bo Regard lifted his head three-quarters of an inch and opened both eyes, before closing them again with a doggy yawn.

Hunter had dangled the bait in front of her and Gaylynn had fallen for it. He'd told her to stay away and she'd come down off the mountain. Just like he'd wanted her to.

And what about that kiss they'd shared? Well, actually, she had started it. But he'd certainly responded. But then what else was a warm-blooded man supposed to do when a wild woman threw herself into his arms? And there was no mistaking the fact that Hunter was *very* warm-blooded. Downright boiling, in fact. At least, that's the way he'd made her feel.

She didn't want to think about her feelings for Hunter. She was confused enough as it was.

"You're clever, I'll give you that," Gaylynn said as she returned the keys to Hunter a short while later.

"Was there something in particular you were referring to," he asked, "or just my general overall intelligence?"

Instead of confronting him with her suspicions, Gaylynn just smiled and kissed his cheek. Seeing the look of total confusion in his eyes did her soul good. In her book, confusion, like misery, loved company. And if her thoughts and emotions were a chaotic riot, then his should be, too. Besides, it had been sweet of him to have gone to all that trouble for her.

Gaylynn was almost out the door when he said, "Wait a second! Ma Battle called looking for you. She'd like you to stop by her place today if you have the time. She's closed up the store for the day. Her house is just a block south, on the corner, right-hand side. She wanted to talk to you about the library's books."

"Okay," Gaylynn said.

Staring after her, Hunter just shook his head and muttered, "Women!"

Ma Battle's home was a sight to behold. The living room had an odd assortment of collectibles on every available surface. In addition, one wall had shelves mounted on it, and they, too, were filled with a variety of books and commemorative plates. The couch had an intricately colorful friendship quilt neatly arranged over the back of it, while the dining room table was piled high with papers and file folders.

"Just some of the Ladies Auxiliary's paperwork," the older woman said. "And, of course, all my contest entries. Despite what Boone said, I *have* won things over the years. Lots of them. After all, even a blind hog finds an acorn now and then."

"Excuse me?"

"A country saying meaning that everyone gets lucky sometime or another. As proof of that, do you see that seashell lamp over yonder? I won that. A lot of these other things are free offers I've gotten—like the glass you're drinking out of." Ma Battle had handed her a glass of iced tea practically the moment Gaylynn had stepped inside. "It's real crystal."

"I couldn't help admiring the quilt you have here on the couch. It's beautiful!"

"Why, thank you kindly. I've made many a quilt in my day. At least one for all of my five children and all my fifteen grandchildren. They don't live 'round these parts now, but they still have my quilts. There's an old mountain saying that if a young girl sleeps under a new quilt, she'll dream of the boy she's going to marry."

A lot less drastic than literally finding love "where you look for it," as ran in her own family, Gaylynn thought to herself with a grin.

"We used to have even more quilting bees than we do now. It's really just an excuse for us all to get together and talk about the goings-on, you're quiltin' and a'talkin' and a'quiltin'..." Her accent got thicker as her face reflected her fond memories. "In the end we have a beautiful quilt to show for it. Each quilt takes on a life of its own ... but I didn't ask you over here to talk quiltin', I asked you so I could show you where the library books are stored. Bessie called and told me you're going to reopen the library."

"With some help," Gaylynn said, the first time she'd been able to get three words in edgewise since she'd arrived.

"I can't wait to get started. What needs to be done first?"

"Cleaning the interior of the building."

"I agree. We could do that this weekend. I'll make sure everyone is there with buckets and mops in hand. The old card catalog is in my spare room. It's a mighty nice oak cabinet with six drawers full of cards. The books themselves are stored in three basements, the three driest basements in town—mine, Hazel Rue's and Lillie Montgomery's."

"You actually got the Rues and the Montgomeries both involved? I thought they were feuding."

"Well, they are, after a sort. Not as bad as the blood feuds in the old days. Not that we were ever as bad here in North Carolina as they were over in Tennessee and Kentucky," she stoutly maintained. "Regardless, I didn't like to play favorites between the two families. So if Lillie got to store books, that meant Hazel did, too."

From which, Gaylynn gathered it was a big honor to be asked to store the library collection. She asked, "How many books are we talking about?"

"I don't rightly know. We never did get around to counting them all. But I'd say I've got about twenty or thirty boxes full and the other two ladies have about the same."

"Then we'll concentrate on preparing the building first, and then we'll start moving the books back. The library would only be open for limited hours. I could be there part of the day and then maybe someone else could take over," Gaylynn said, speaking her thoughts aloud.

"Whatever you think is best."

Unspoken was the question of what would happen to the library once Gaylynn returned to Chicago. Gaylynn had been involved with community projects before, she knew that often all that was needed was someone to jump-start things. Then, once the project was nearing completion, the local people could take over and run things themselves. That had happened in Chicago's neighborhoods when Gaylynn had done volunteer work there. And that's what would happen here in Lonesome Gap. They'd do just fine without her.

But would she be fine without them?

* * *

"So how are things going down there?" Gaylynn's sister-in-law, Brett, asked.

"Fine," Gaylynn said automatically. She'd called Brett on the cellular phone because she desperately needed a woman her own age to talk to.

"Are you keeping busy?"

"You could say that. I've taken in a mama cat and her two kittens. But don't tell Michael or *he'll* have kittens. They're housebroken now and got a clean bill of health from the vet not two hours ago." As she spoke, Gaylynn smiled down at Blue and Spook, who were curled up sleeping near Cleo. All three felines had serene smiles of utter contentment. Gaylynn had never seen cats smile before. "You should see them, Brett. They're the cutest little things."

"Is it my imagination or are you getting a Southern accent?" Brett asked.

"It must be your imagination."

"So what else have you been doing, besides setting up a house for wayward cats and their kittens?"

Gaylynn decided against telling Brett about the library reopening. After all, no action had been taken yet. She'd wait and see what happened during the clean-up operation on Saturday before bringing anything up. Instead, she said, "Actually, I've been doing some sketching, which is sort of strange considering the fact that I never had an ounce of artistic talent before. Must be the inspirational surroundings here in the mountains."

"Or it could be the Rom box," Brett stated. "Remember how you said Michael was no good around babies before? After he got the box, he was great with

Hope. And not only that, now everywhere we go babies reach out to him. It's really something to see.''

"And you think the box might be helping me sketch? But why? There was a practical purpose to Michael's being good with a baby. It helped bring the two of you together.'' Gaylynn couldn't believe she was actually talking about magic so matter-of-factly. But then she had been raised to believe in possibilities.

"I'm not sure why sketching is important for you,'' Brett replied. "Only *you* can know that. Has it changed anything for you?''

"It has made me notice things more,'' Gaylynn admitted. "To see the small beauties in life. When you draw something you have to really *look* at it, you know what I mean?'' While talking on the cellular phone, Gaylynn had doodled on a blank sheet of paper. The lines and circles quickly became Hunter's craggy face, reminding her of the main purpose of this call. "Uh, actually I'm phoning you because I need another woman's opinion.''

"Man trouble?'' Brett inquired, her voice sympathetic.

"Yes. You know, that's one of the things I like so much about you,'' Gaylynn declared. "You're really tuned in to people and their feelings. You were even able to figure Michael out, and heaven knows, he's kind of complicated.''

"You can say that again,'' Brett agreed with a laugh. "But then I had some Rom magic helping me along. Is that what happened to you? Are you having man trouble because of the charmed box?''

"I wish it were that easy.''

"Uh-oh," Brett murmured. "What happened when you opened the box? You *have* opened it by now, haven't you?"

"Sure. And nothing happened."

"You didn't see anyone when you opened it?"

"I saw some derelict old guy dressed like a bum hiking through the woods. He could have been a moonshiner for all I know."

"Oh, no!"

"But luckily I don't think he saw me. The good news is that I haven't seen him since. The bad news is that I've got . . . feelings . . . for someone else."

"Who?"

"Hunter Davis."

"Michael's old friend?"

"That's right. And I don't know what to do about it."

"What seems to be the problem? Is he married or already involved with someone else?"

"No. He's divorced now, although Michael never bothered to tell me that."

"I'm still working on your brother's communication skills," Brett ruefully acknowledged.

"Where is he, by the way? I know he would be growling like a bear in the background if he were home."

"He's taken Hope out in her stroller for a walk."

"Good. Then you can give me some womanly advice without him eavesdropping. What should I do about Hunter?"

"Why don't you tell me what the problem seems to be?"

Brett's question made Gaylynn realized that there was no way she could do that, without confessing about the mugging and her real reasons for taking that leave of absence from her teaching position. And if Brett knew, she'd have to tell Michael. Which meant Gaylynn had to skirt the issue somewhat. "It's just that...I guess you could say that I'm kind of in the middle of this mid-life crisis right now and I don't know what I'm going to do with my life. I'm on leave from my job—I'm not sure what I want to do about anything. It feels like I don't know who I am anymore."

"When you say you're not sure what you want to do about anything anymore, does that include Hunter?"

"I'm tempted to just stay in his arms forever," Gaylynn confessed with an unsteady laugh.

"What would be wrong with that?"

"A lot of things. The fact that he might not feel the same way about me as I feel about him. The fact that he may just be looking out for me because I'm his best friend's baby sister and Michael asked him to. Hunter always was a sucker for the underdog or anyone needing help. And then there's the fact that he's a police officer."

"And all those things scare you?"

"Spitless."

"There were a lot of maybes in there," Brett stated dryly. "Maybe Hunter *does* feel the same way about you. Have you thought of that?"

"Lately I have, yes. That's why I'm calling you."

"What about the fact that Hunter is a police officer? Does that bother you?"

"Not so much bother as *scare*. I know all the logical arguments, that we're in a quiet little town in North Carolina, that we're not talking the kind of danger that a policeman in Chicago would be exposed to. But still... Oh, God, I hate this feeling of being such a chicken!"

"I haven't known you all that long," Brett acknowledged, "but I wouldn't describe you as a chicken. Everyone else in the family describes you as the fearless one."

"That was before. How would you describe me?"

"Maybe as someone who's temporarily lost their way."

"Bingo," Gaylynn whispered unsteadily.

"Do you want to talk about it?"

"Not now. But thanks for asking."

"You're welcome. And the offer remains open. If there's a time that you want tell me more, you just give me a call."

"I will."

"Which still leaves us the dilemma of Hunter. Are you in love with him?"

"You get right to the point, don't you?"

"No point in wasting your money—this call is on your dime," Brett teased her. "So what's your answer?"

"I loved Hunter when I was thirteen. I had a terrible crush on him. He's five years older than I am. He went to the police academy, worked as a Chicago cop, got married and eventually moved away."

"And you forgot about him?"

"Sort of. At least, I told myself I had. Now I'm not so sure. I think maybe I've compared all the men I've met over the years to Hunter."

"And the others never quite stacked up, huh?"

"How could you tell that?"

"From the sound of your voice. You've got a very expressive voice, you know. And when you say Hunter's name it sounds like..."

"I'm in love with him? I am. It's kind of scary saying it out loud, though," Gaylynn admitted with a nervous laugh. "This is the first time I've actually done that."

"Scary doesn't even come close," Brett said. "I was *petrified* the first time I said the words out loud. And then I made the mistake of doing so right next to the baby monitor, so your brother overheard me."

"But you two fell in love at first sight."

"Yes, we did. But we didn't recognize it at the time. It's too bad Hunter wasn't the one you saw when you first opened that box. Have you tried opening the box again?"

"Hunter held it in his hands the other night. He said he didn't notice anything unusual about it."

"Did you notice anything?"

"I can't even think straight when Hunter is around," Gaylynn confessed as the newly awakened Blue and Spook wound around her ankles for a petting.

"If you feel that way about Hunter, what's to stop you from going after what you want?" Brett asked her.

At the moment, the usually skittish Spook took it into her head to chase after a startled Blue. The sight of the pursued turning around and becoming the pursuer gave Gaylynn an idea—what if she were to stop running away from her fears and were instead to chase after what she wanted?

"I mean, you'll never know until you try, right?" Brett was saying. "Gaylynn, are you still there?"

"I'm still here," she said. "And I got one of those moments of revelation, you know the kind where a light bulb snaps on over your head. I know what I'm going to do now."

"Good. You want to tell me?"

"I'm going to seduce Hunter Davis. Got any suggestions for me?"

Saturday morning Gaylynn arrived at the library to find a small crowd gathered there already. As she was fast learning, two dozen people constituted a crowd in a town as small as Lonesome Gap.

A few picnic tables were set up in front of the library's redbrick building. The yellow tablecloths flapping in the brisk breeze were prevented from flying off thanks to some heavy rocks strategically placed on the corners. Several women were pouring coffee and handing out muffins. Gaylynn recognized Floyd and Bessie Twitty, along with their grandson, Boone. Ma Battle and Darlene, the waitress from the café, were serving the coffee and muffins. The two older men who had asked her if she'd wanted to join the pool were busy supervising a bunch of kids who were pulling weeds. Overall, there was a sense of organized chaos.

Hunter was there, too. Gaylynn sensed his presence before actually seeing him. The wind ruffled his hair, increasing its shaggy appearance. A pair of aviator-style sunglasses hid his deep-set eyes, but there was no hiding the devilish slash of his smile.

"I wasn't sure if I'd see you here today," Gaylynn said.

"I wouldn't miss it for the world. Come on, there are a few people I'd like you to meet."

The few turned out to be more than a dozen, all of them related to Hunter in one way or another. Try as she did to keep track, one smiling face blended into another. Jeff, Jerry, Noah and at least three Jimmies.

"How many cousins do you have in this town?" she asked Hunter after meeting what seemed like the twentieth one.

"Not as many as I used to," Hunter replied. "A lot of them have moved away. Now there are only about fifteen or so left."

"And I thought *I* came from a large family," Gaylynn murmured with a shake of her head.

"I'm the odd one in the clan, without any brothers or sisters."

"But you've got enough cousins to make up for that, and then some."

"Did you notice the family resemblance?"

"I didn't talk to them long enough to see if they were as full of blarney as you are," Gaylynn retorted with a sassy grin.

"Is that any way to speak to a lawman?" he demanded.

His grin was as lawless as they came. Dressed in a light blue shirt and black jeans, it was easy for her to forget what he did for a living. Instead, she let herself be charmed by the humor in his eyes as he teased her about getting cobwebs in her hair while cleaning.

Three hours later, the cobwebs were all gone. After the worst of the dirt and grime had been taken care of, the front and back doors to the building had been left open to air the place out. The Ladies Auxiliary League had brought enough buckets and wood soap to transform the hardwood floor into a gleaming showpiece. The bookshelves had been likewise washed down and were ready for books. Vinegar had been applied to the glass windows until they shone.

"It's starting to look good," Gaylynn noted approvingly.

"I'll tell you what's looking good," Darlene replied from beside her. "Hunter." He and one of his young cousins were moving a bookcase on the other side of the library. Since the sun was heating things up considerably, both men had taken off their shirts. "If I weren't a married woman...whew!" Darlene drew her arm across her forehead. "Lordy, Hunter has this sexy laid-back attitude that just about makes your insides melt, y'know what I mean?"

"Yeah, I know what you mean," Gaylynn agreed, fanning herself with a paper towel. A second later she rubbed her itchy nose, no doubt caused by all the dust they'd stirred up today.

Seeing her, Darlene said, "Your nose bothering you? You know they say that an itching nose means you should expect company."

Gaylynn was hoping she'd have company real soon—Hunter's company. As if granting her wish, when the announcement came from outside that lunch was ready, Hunter tugged his shirt back on and joined her in line.

The picnic tables out front had been transformed into a veritable smorgasbord. Everyone had brought something—a hot covered dish of chicken and noodles or beef stew, homemade corn relish, sugar-cured ham, sausages, tomato salad, jugs full of fresh-squeezed lemonade and at least five pies—three of them peach. Gaylynn noticed that Bo Regard had positioned himself beneath one of the picnic tables so that should any tasty morsels drop down, he wouldn't have to move much to eat them.

While the volunteers ate, someone brought out a dulcimer and started playing it. The music, the ever-present mountains, the lush greenery lit by dappled sunlight, the sweet scent of flowers and freshly mowed grass, all conspired to create a scene of utter perfection. These people might not have all the latest conveniences or gold credit cards, but they had a strong sense of community and a love for the land that had gone sadly lacking in too many other places. Gaylynn had to blink away sudden tears. But they were happy tears, not sad ones.

"You okay?" Hunter asked, putting an arm around her shoulder as he scooted closer on the picnic bench they were seated on.

Gaylynn nodded. "You know I've heard bagpipers in Scotland and zithers in the Alps and now the dulcimer in the Blue Ridge—"

"And a fiddle," Hunter said as Floyd picked up a lovingly battered-looking instrument and started to play.

"And each time I get a lump in my throat at the sheer beauty of it," Gaylynn stated.

"Must be a girl thing," Hunter decided.

Her elbow was in his rib cage before he knew what hit him.

"Sorry," she said with a sassy smile that made him want to snatch her in his arms and kiss her. "You were saying?"

Hunter decided that, discretion being the better part of valor, he wouldn't risk repeating his earlier comment.

He was rewarded for his prudence by having her ask him, "What are you doing tonight?"

"Working," he replied. "Why?"

"How about tomorrow evening? Are you working then?

"No. Why?"

"I thought maybe I'd invite you to dinner at my place. A special dinner. Your favorite fried chicken. What would you say to that?"

"Are you only *maybe* as in possibly-it-could-happen inviting me? Or is this a real, bona fide, honest-to-goodness invitation?"

"The latter," she replied.

"In that case, I accept."

"Good," she said briskly. "Come by at seven."

By six fifty-five the next evening, Hunter was striding up the steps to her front door. Hell, he'd already killed ten minutes back at his own cabin by changing his shirt three times. He'd never been so flustered in all his life.

Which was ridiculous. It was just Gaylynn, he reminded himself as he straightened his tie before knocking on the door. "I'll be right there. Hold on a minute," he heard Gaylynn shout.

He shouldn't have come five minutes early. He sat down in the rocking chair on the porch and tried to calm himself. It didn't work. He watched the second hand on his watch ticking off the seconds and waited for Gaylynn to open the door.

What was going on? Getting up, he knocked again. "I'm coming!" she claimed.

A few seconds later the door opened and his jaw fell!

Eight

Gaylynn had been rushing around all afternoon, trying to prepare for this novel occasion. Little had gone right. She'd planned a special meal, but her first attempt at preparing it had gotten sidetracked when Blue had stolen a chicken leg off the table.

Unfortunately, the rest of the chicken—which Gaylynn had been trying to fry—had practically gone up in flames when she'd somehow gotten too much flour into the hot skillet. It had been all she could do to prevent the fire from spreading before she'd smothered it with a lid. As it was, she'd burned two kitchen towels to a crisp. There was no saving the chicken.

In all the commotion, it was only natural that Gaylynn forgot all about the pie that was in the oven. By the time she realized where the rest of the smoke was coming from, it, too, was a goner.

By then the cabin had smelled as badly as if *it* had gone up in smoke instead of the hapless meal. Gaylynn had thrown open all the windows and hastily waved her large sketch pad in the hope of creating a breeze. As luck would have it, the stiff wind of yesterday had completely disappeared.

Frantic now because she had nothing else to cook for dinner, and she'd promised Hunter fried chicken, Gaylynn had called the Lonesome Café and Hazel's Hash House to see if they had take-out fried chicken. The former was closed on Sundays and the latter only served chicken on weeknights. But Ma Battle always did up a batch of fried chicken on Sundays they'd told her.

A call to Ma Battle had confirmed that. Desperate, Gaylynn had offered to buy the dinner, but Ma Battle had insisted on donating it "to the cause" as she put it.

Her hair still in rag curlers—because there hadn't been time to mess with a curling iron, and besides, she'd left it back in Chicago—Gaylynn had hopped into her trusty red car... only to have it stall on her twice on the way down the hill.

Then she'd had to wait at the one-way cement bridge while some idiot tried to fish off it. Recognizing "the idiot" as Boone Twitty, she impatiently beeped her horn to hurry him along. With a grin and a wave, Boone just kept right on reeling in the fish he'd caught.

She'd finally made it to Ma Battle's and even managed to load all the goodies for dinner without spilling anything.

"You might try waving the platter of fried chicken in the air a few times to make the place smell like you've been cooking up a storm," the older woman suggested with a twinkle in her eyes.

"It already smells like I've been cooking up—a *fi-restorm*," Gaylynn replied in exasperation.

"And mess up the kitchen a mite to make it look like you slaved in it all day."

"Trust me, the kitchen is already messed up," Gaylynn declared. "I'm just lucky it didn't burn to a crisp the way my dinner did."

"Now don't you worry none, that happened to me on more than one occasion when I was young," Ma Battle said. "You just do what I did, smile sweetly and rub a little chicken grease behind one ear. Here's the last of it," she said, handing over a bowl of mashed potatoes. "I wrapped everything in aluminum foil to keep it hot for you."

"But what are you going to eat?"

"Now don't you worry about me none. I aim on eating the rest of the ham I made last night."

"Thanks," Gaylynn said, giving the woman a grateful hug. "You're a real sweetie to help me out this way. You're sure I can't pay for it . . . ?"

"Nonsense. You and Hunter have a nice time."

Gaylynn made it home by six-forty five. The dinner was safely covered on the counter; the cats were sacked out on the bed, their little and not-so-little tummies filled with a can of tuna fish.

Now it was time for Gaylynn to replace her work clothes with a very special outfit. The button-front jacquard dress was the essence of romance, or so the salesclerk had told her when Gaylynn had bought it last year. The tea-rose color suited her, while the cap sleeves and full, ankle-sweeping skirt made her feel elegant and confident.

Actually, she had no idea how the dress had ended up in her suitcase. It wasn't something she'd planned on bringing, but somehow it had shown up in the tumble of casual clothes she'd tossed into her bag. Maybe it was destiny. Or even a bit of Rom magic. Whatever, the dress was perfect for what she had in mind for this evening. Seduction!

She'd barely tugged the dress over her head when she heard a knock at the front door. Oh, no, Hunter was early!

"I'll be right there," she called out. "Hold on a minute."

Gaylynn had done her makeup before leaving for Ma Battle's, thank goodness, but she still had those darned rag curlers wrapped up in her hair. Working at the speed of light, she undid them, letting her hair fall into curly disarray. Yanking up her long skirt, she dashed into the bathroom to check her appearance. It would have to do, she decided while hastily brushing her hair as best she could. The natural look was in, right?

Another knock on the door. "I'm coming," she said.

As she passed by the Rom box, Gaylynn paused to open it and remove the medallion from inside. Feeling the need of a little courage, she pinned it on her dress for good luck before taking a deep breath and opening the door.

Hunter stared at her. Instead of looking at her with that customary gleam of humor in his eyes—which often made her wonder if he was laughing at her or trying to seduce her—his expression was one of astonished wonder.

Her heart sank. Had she gotten *too* dressed up for the occasion? Was she making a total idiot of herself? Were her intentions written all over her face as boldly as the lipstick she'd had to reapply four times before she'd gotten it on right?

Well, too bad if Hunter was astonished, she decided. She wasn't about to back out now. Not after all the trouble she'd gone to!

Taking him by the arm, she tugged him inside—just in case he got any ideas of taking off. "You're early."

"You're gorgeous," Hunter said huskily, his mountain drawl even more apparent than usual.

Instead of being flustered by his compliment, Gaylynn gained courage from it. "Thank you," she replied.

"Something smells good," he added.

"The fried chicken?" she suggested hopefully.

"No, this smells more like..." He paused to sniff.

Don't let him say burnt embers or charcoal, she prayed.

"Peaches," he stated triumphantly.

"It might be the pie." Ma Battle had added a peach pie along with the dinner.

Stepping closer, he murmured, "No, it's your hair."

Gaylynn had almost forgotten the peach shampoo and shower gel she'd used earlier. Apparently, it worked better on Hunter than Ma Battle's suggestion of a little chicken grease might have, she noted with silent humor.

Seeing Gaylynn's secret smile, Hunter was hard-pressed not to yank her into his arms and kiss her senseless. She looked all peaches and cream in that dress. Her skin was slightly flushed, her lipstick glossy and wet—making him long to see if she tasted as good as she looked.

But she was already bustling away toward the kitchen. "Dinner is ready now, if you're ready to eat?" she asked.

"I'm *ready*," Hunter muttered hoarsely.

She got the impression he wasn't talking about eating. Good! Judging by his initial reaction to her appearance, step one in her seduction plan had worked. She'd made an impression, or at least the dress had. She'd deliberately left half the buttons on the dress's full skirt undone, allowing her to flash a great deal of leg as she sauntered back and forth from the kitchen to place Ma Battle's excellently prepared meal on the table.

"Is that everything we'll need?" she asked, trying to remember if she'd forgotten anything.

Draping a paper napkin over his lap, as much to hide his reaction to Gaylynn's shapely thighs as for etiquette's sake, Hunter tried not to stare at her partially undone dress.

Should he mention the fact that half the buttons were unfastened? Was that his fault, because he'd surprised her by showing up a bit early? If so, he wasn't about to point it out. She might take it into her head to button up those buttons, and frankly, he was enjoying the view much too much to have her do that at this point.

"Would you prefer a thigh or a breast?" she asked.

His eyes went from Gaylynn's shapely legs to her equally shapely chest. The dress's sweetheart neckline gave him a partial view of the shadowy valley between her breasts. His nostrils flared at the scent of peaches drifting from the warmth of her skin.

"Thigh or breast?" she repeated.

"Both look great," he replied, his gaze remaining fixed on her body and not the food she was offering. "Downright mouthwatering, in fact."

"I'm so glad you think so," she said with a smile before bending over to slide two pieces of chicken on his plate—one breast and one thigh.

The possibility that she'd purposely left those buttons undone was definitely starting to occur to him. Was this her way of showing her appreciation for the way he'd supposedly helped her? Gaylynn had never been one to let a debt go unpaid.

"How's your chicken?" she asked him.

He had to sample a bite before replying. "Fine. Great!"

"I'm glad you like it."

"Tastes remarkably like Ma Battle's fried chicken," he said appreciatively. "And she makes the best fried chicken in the state."

"Does she?" Feeling as if she was getting into slippery ground, she changed the subject. "So how was work today?"

"Fine. We had a little excitement last night, but then that's to be expected on a Saturday night."

Her heart sank. "What happened?"

"There was a call about a disturbance, a bunch of guys had a little too much to drink. They were in the middle of the street, shouting and arguing. Most of them dispersed when I showed up and told them to go on home, but one guy was being a real pain in the butt. The disturbance was in front of his house, so basically all he'd done was go stand in his front yard and keep yelling. I told him to go inside or I'd arrest him."

"And then what happened?"

"He went inside, only to open the downstairs window, lean out and begin shouting obscenities again. Bragged about how he was safe because he was inside his house and no one could do anything about it. He was raising all kinds of Cain, waking all the neighbors up. Finally I'd had it."

"What did you do?"

"Walked up to the guy, grabbed him by his shirt-front and dragged him out through the open window. 'Appears to me you're outside *now*,' I told him, before arresting him."

"Isn't that illegal or something?"

"No, it's happens once a month with this guy. It's like a ritual we go through. It's Bobby Ray's idea of entertainment."

Not knowing what to say, Gaylynn just smiled and fingered the medallion she wore. Her actions drew his attention once again to the sweetheart neckline of her dress. Touching the medallion lessened her uneasiness and increased her sassiness. Discreetly throwing back her shoulders, she leaned forward and huskily asked, "So, would you care for another breast?"

Hunter wondered what she'd do if he just reached out and caressed her breast . . . before cursing himself as a mannerless fool. She hadn't fingered that strange pin she was wearing on purpose, had she? To get his attention? She was just being polite. Wasn't she?

There was a certain gleam in her eye that made him wonder . . .

After dinner, she served coffee and slices of peach pie on the coffee table in front of the couch. She'd put a blue-and-white gingham cover over the piece of furniture, which made it look downright cozy. Despite that, there was no denying the fact that the center cushion was dented, rolling Hunter and Gaylynn toward each other. But for once she was glad of the couch's strange idiosyncracies.

With every minute that passed, Gaylynn felt more and more confident about her decision to seduce Hunter. He was the man she'd been saving herself for all these years. In light of the embrace they'd shared in front of the library the other day, and his reaction to her tonight, she decided there was a darn good chance that he was attracted to her, as well.

Brushing her shoulder against his as she leaned forward to replace her coffee cup on the table, she was delighted to feel the heat of his body and the slight quickening of his breath.

She was getting to him! Hallelujah!

The distant sound of thunder reverberating across the mountains echoed the pounding of her heart.

"Do you still love thunderstorms like you did as a kid?" he asked her.

She nodded. "My father used to tell me that thunder was the sound of God snoring."

Hunter just nodded, distracted as he was by the sight of her daintily licking a bit of peach syrup from her upper lip. She'd missed a spot. His self-discipline, which had been stretched to the limit all night, suddenly snapped.

Unable to resist a second longer, he reached out to wipe his index finger across the delicate curve of her lip. A moment later his mouth replaced his finger as he tenderly, yet fiercely, claimed her as his. The kiss was part possession, part pure passion.

Gaylynn welcomed his demands and returned them in equal measure. All the reasons why she shouldn't be doing this were far outweighed by all the reasons why she should. This felt so right, perfect, meant-to-be.

The anticipation was building as the distant thunder rolled closer. Closer, too, rolled his fingers—over the curve of her breasts until he brushed his thumb across one rosy crest. She arched her back in excitement. Before she knew what had happened, with one smooth move he had her laid out on the couch.

Now they were pressed together from shoulder to thigh. The hunger continued to build and with it the need to be closer still. His tie was dispatched with first. The buttons on her dress came next. His prowling fingers then focused their attention on the front fastener of her lacy bra. Her gasp of undisguised pleasure coincided with the first brush of his fingertips against her now bare breasts. He caressed her gently, almost reverently at first.

Without further urging, her nipples hardened for him. Her response seemed to fascinate him, for he focused his attention on their rosy nubs, lowering his head to tease her with the wet tip of his tongue, before closing his lips around her. The sweet suction was nearly her undoing.

Imbedding her fingers in his thick hair, she pressed him to her. Ribbons of hot desire uncurled deep within her womb.

Something sharp dug into her back, so sharp there was no ignoring it. "Ouch!" she exclaimed.

Hunter immediately pulled her upright. "What's wrong?"

Looking over her shoulder, she yanked at the offending item with one hand, while trying to hold her clothing in place with the other. "It's a stupid pin. I guess it must have been left over from when I redid the couch cushion." She felt like an idiot. "Nothing like having a pin burst your bubble, huh?" she muttered, her hair falling over her face and shielding her expression from his view.

"I wouldn't say that. Things are definitely still all pumped up," he assured her with a naughty grin. "Feel." Gently taking her hand in his, he pressed it against his arousal.

"Hunter, make love to me," she whispered as he kissed her again.

He paused, leaning far enough away to gaze into her eyes. "Are you sure that's what you want? This isn't just gratitude or something..."

"Why should I feel grateful to you?" she huskily demanded in between seductive kisses along the stubborn line of his jaw. "All you've done is get me all hot and bothered and then not done anything about it."

With that, he tugged her off the couch and up into his arms.

Shrieking in surprise, she put her arms around his neck. Her dress was still open, her bra undone, leaving her breasts bare as she rubbed against his chest.

"Is that more romantic for you?" he asked. This time his smile was downright wolfish as he carried her into the bedroom.

The storm had sent the cats scampering from her bed to the dark safety of the closet, where they'd hid the last time there had been a storm like this.

Actually, there had never been a storm like this—the one raging inside of Gaylynn was unparalleled, proving to her that Hunter was the only man for her, the one she'd been waiting for all her life.

As he set her in the middle of the bed, Gaylynn remembered the package of latex condoms sitting bold-as-brass on the bedside table. Brett had sent them by overnight priority mail along with a note:

> Your brother would probably shoot me if he knew I was sending these to you, but Lonesome Gap sounds small and I didn't think you'd want to shop there for these. Remember, if you need to talk, I'm right at the other end of the phone.

Bessie probably would have had a heart attack had she known what was in the priority package she'd handed Gaylynn the day before.

As it was, Gaylynn was the one having a heart attack as Hunter stroked the palm of his hand from her shoulder to her navel. Her clothes, aside from her panties, were now gone—how had that happened? All that remained was the warmth of his skin against hers. She loved the feel of his hands on her. There was nothing like it, no words to explain it. Delicious. Better than anything she'd ever experienced before.

She wondered if touching him would feel as good. It did. She relished the freedom to explore, feeling as if she'd unlocked a treasure chest of wonders. The long indention of his spine, the curve of his shoulder, the contour of every muscle, the hard resilience of his flesh beneath her hands—all these filled her with awe. And raw excitement.

His shirt and slacks had gone the way of her dress, melting away, like the mists that flowed across the mountains. Thunder boomed overhead and lightning flashed through the white priscilla curtains she'd made to cover the window.

The lights in the living room went out, plunging the cabin into total darkness aside from the frequent flashes of lightning, but Gaylynn barely noticed because now nothing separated them. He trailed his hand over her hip, down her thigh, back up again before dipping into her. Just a butterfly-light probing to start. Seeing and feeling her pleasure, he increased his teasing seduction. One finger, then two, rubbing, pressing, sliding—driving her wild with yearning.

"Do you know the real danger in a storm like this?" he whispered in her ear, taking the time to nibble on her earlobe in between every third word.

"No, what?"

"Live wires." He moved against her, showing her exactly what he meant.

"Really?" She took him in her hand, stroking his throbbing hardness with her loving fingers.

"*Very* live wires," he growled, reaching over to grab the box of condoms.

The moment he was sheathed, she murmured, "I know where you can plug that in." She reached for him and guided him to the moist entrance aching for him. "Right here... yes... oh!"

Their eyes met as his body merged with hers. He came into her with one powerful thrust, too late realizing the virginal barrier there.

She flinched at the brief moment of burning discomfort.

Hunter froze, his entire body rigid.

She could see the stunned disbelief on his face.

"Don't stop now," she whispered, lifting her hips when he would have withdrawn.

He would have asked questions but his mind wasn't functioning. Her tightness surrounding him had short-circuited his brain, leaving him on the brink of prematurely climaxing.

Drawing forth every ounce of willpower, he slowly moved within her, watching her face for any further sign of discomfort. Instead, he saw dawning realization, anticipation, increasing pleasure.

Using every ounce of skill and care at his command, Hunter tried to make it good for her. He lasted as long as he could. Unable to hold out any longer, he reached down to where they were joined, seeking the sensitive nub hidden in her nest of curls. Brushing it with his thumb, he watched and felt her reach her climax. The flush of color on her face, the wide-eyed look of passion, her dainty breathless scream gave him a thrilling sense of fulfillment even before he reached his own matching satisfaction.

"Shh, you'll wake him up."

After all that had happened the night before, Hunter couldn't believe he'd fallen asleep.

He'd fully intended to talk to Gaylynn last night after they'd made love, but somehow, while trying to think of the right thing to say to her, he'd closed his eyes for a few minutes. The next thing he knew, it was morning.

Granted, he hadn't gotten much sleep lately, what with the extra hours he'd been putting in at work, but still . . .

"Don't jump on him," Hunter heard Gaylynn caution.

A second later eight pounds of Siamese cat landed on top of him. Since he was lying on his back, Cleo came dangerously close to emasculating him as she dug in her claws through the top sheet in some feline show of revenge.

He jackknifed to an upright position, which did dislodge the cat but not before she used him as a launching pad, all twenty of her claws out.

"You scared her," Gaylynn chastised him as Cleo went shooting past her into the living room.

"Yeah, well, the feeling was mutual," he growled.

Mutual feeling. Was that what they'd shared last night? she wondered. She knew she loved him. But his feelings for her were still something of a mystery to her. Had it just been physical desire on his part?

"We need to talk," he muttered, watching her with brooding eyes.

"Okay," she said agreeably, sitting on the edge of the bed while she nibbled on a piece of rye bread toast slathered with apple butter.

He started by saying, "Why didn't you tell me... Why haven't you ever...?"

"Celibacy is in, haven't you heard?" she replied, shooting him a bold grin.

"I'm serious."

"So am I. Believe me, there are a lot more of us virgins around these days."

"Well, there's one *less* virgin around today."

"Yeah," she agreed, munching on another bite of toast. "Are you hungry?"

Looking at her made him hungry all right, but not for food.

When he didn't answer her question, she sighed and said, "Look, my birthday is only a month away. Maybe I just decided that I didn't want to be a thirty-year-old virgin."

Hunter was not amused. "I don't believe you. You're not the kind of woman to share something like this with a man you don't... love."

The look on his face was not that of a man in love,
a man who planned on spending the rest of his life with
her, a man bent on marriage. The look on his face was
that of a man with regrets. He said, "If I'd known you
were a . . . that is, that you hadn't . . ."

"The word is virgin," she supplied in exasperation.

"Where do you think this . . . relationship . . . is going?" he abruptly demanded.

"Where do *you* think it's going?" she countered.

"No place," he replied. "I mean, you'll be going
back to Chicago soon and I'll be staying here."

"Right," she said, even though it felt wrong. Very
wrong. She and Hunter were meant to be together. But
she couldn't hit the man over the head with her decla-
ration of love and make him return her feelings. But
she could make sure he had no regrets about what
they'd shared last night. And she'd do or say whatever
it took to make sure that their lovemaking was not a
one-time occurrence. "Look, let's not complicate this
any more than necessary, okay? No pressure. We'll just
enjoy each other's company while we can."

"Enjoy how?" he asked, wanting further clarifica-
tion. "Like we did last night?"

She nodded, refusing to look away from the direct
challenge in his eyes. "What do you say? Deal?" She
held out her hand.

To her relief, he shook it. "Deal."

But even as Hunter agreed, his inner feelings remained in a turmoil. He knew he felt more than just
passion for Gaylynn, but was it love? Who could tell?

And then there was the undeniable fact that he was
hardly a prize for a woman like Gaylynn—the smartest
woman he'd ever known, someone who'd traveled
around the world. His ex-wife had barely graduated

from high school and she'd never left the city of Chicago until he'd brought her down to Lonesome Gap, a godforsaken flea-bitten hellhole, as she'd called it on her better days.

Granted, Gaylynn seemed to get a kick out of his little hometown; she thought it was quaint. For now. But that would eventually wear off, it always did with newcomers. They ended up moving someplace not so far off the beaten path, a town that was up-and-coming rather than one struggling to stay alive.

He could see that Gaylynn was rapidly recovering from the attack that had sent her fleeing to the sanctuary of these mountains. He'd been right when he'd thought that her condition of uncertainty and fear was only a temporary one, a natural reaction to the trauma she'd gone through. But already her inherent courage was returning. He could see it increasing every day. Hell, the fact that she'd taken it upon herself to seduce him was proof of that.

Not that he needed much seducing; he'd been fighting his feelings for her for some time now. Even so, Hunter was still sure that nothing would stop her from returning to her old life in Chicago. She'd just said so herself. He'd asked if she would be going back to her old life, and she'd said yes.

Gaylynn watched the shadows flickering in Hunter's deep-set green eyes and wished she could do something to erase them. She didn't want him feeling badly about what had happened. She'd had her eyes wide open when she'd started out last night. She hadn't been naive enough to think that after they made love he'd fall to his knees and propose to her. She wasn't even sure she wanted him to. This was all so new and fresh, she didn't want to risk losing the happiness she had by examining it too closely.

Her fingers curled around his, reminding him that he was still holding on to her hand after their handshake of a minute ago. He couldn't resist tugging her back down on top of him and kissing the apple butter from her lips.

When she was lying beside him, he murmured, "You have the most incredible eyes."

"They're just brown."

He shook his head in disagreement. "Dark, liquid eyes are incredibly sexy, don't you know that?"

"I'm rather partial to green eyes myself," she admitted. She was so close to him that she could see the way his eyelashes cast shadows on his skin.

"How partial?" he asked, a devilish light entered his eyes.

"Why don't you let me show you . . ."

"Where do you want me to put this one?" Boone asked Gaylynn as he carried yet another box of books into the library building. First, he'd had to step over Bo Regard, who'd taken to hanging out—or visiting, as the locals called it—on the threshold of the library.

"Let me just open the lid and see what we've got here . . ." Gaylynn replied.

"These are from the Rues' basement," Boone added, as if that might give her a hint of where the books should go.

"Ah, these are the fiction hardcovers. Set the box down over near Stella there and she can unpack them and put them on the shelf."

Boone looked more than happy to comply with Gaylynn's request.

"I ain't seen anyone move that fast since Floyd was chased up a tree by a bear at the age of ten. Floyd was ten, not the bear," Ma Battle felt the need to clarify. She was helping Gaylynn organize all the boxes of books that had been delivered so far, as well as make the important decision of where to place the card catalog. "Makes a body wonder if Stella Rue being such an attractive girl didn't hurry Boone along some."

Seeing the star-struck look on the young man's face, Gaylynn couldn't help wondering the same thing. Stella Rue had come in near the tail end of the clean-up operation on the Saturday before and had volunteered to help out where she could. She was a soft-spoken girl, with lots of freckles and a gentle manner. Gaylynn had liked her right away. So had Boone.

"No good can come of it," Ma Battle said.

"Why's that?" Gaylynn asked.

"Because Boone's mama was a Montgomery, that's why."

"But his last name is Twitty."

"Because his daddy was a Twitty. But his mama was a Montgomery."

"Surely you don't approve of this ongoing feud, do you?" Gaylynn asked the older woman.

"I try not to take sides," she replied. "And you'd be best to do the same. Neither family is known for their quiet nature."

"What are they known for?"

"For their great moonshine. But that was in the old days. Making fine whiskey was a fine art in those times," she noted fondly, "but now it's a lost art."

"Why is that?"

"There are easier jobs to be had these days. I'm not saying moonshining has completely died out—there may be an odd one here or there—but the appreciation of moonshining for the quality of the product itself is a thing of the past."

"You sound as if you're speaking with some authority."

"I should. My granddaddy was one of the best moonshiners in the state. He used to hide the cases of moonshine in the load of corn he'd haul to the city. Truth was, there was lots more moonshine than ears of corn in his truck. Prohibition was in force at the time, making the demand for good whiskey real high."

"Did he ever get caught?"

"No. But getting caught is what started the feud between the Rues and the Montgomeries."

"So I heard," Gaylynn said. "But that was so long ago. Boone doesn't seem to be holding on to any ill feeling toward Stella even though she is a Rue."

"Boone's thinking with his heart instead of his head. Bessie and Floyd would have a fit if they knew which way the wind was blowing."

As the week progressed, the "wind" blew more and more in the direction of Boone and Stella being in the painful throes of young love.

Gaylynn knew because she recognized all the signs, being in the midst of them herself. Not that Hunter had ever looked at her with such a gaze of star-struck awe, although he'd come pretty close that night she'd sprayed a can of whipped cream all over his body and proceeded to lick it off. Yes, he had indeed appeared to be awed. So was she—by the power of her love for Hunter, which grew every moment of every day.

Even now, on a Saturday afternoon, surrounded by half a dozen kids, she still had a hard time keeping her mind off Hunter. The man was downright addictive!

"Teacher, which story are you gonna read us?" one of the children asked, tugging on the skirt of her lilac dress. The cotton knit was easy to clean and one she'd worn often to school back in Chicago. It made for a nice change from all the jeans and T-shirts she'd been wearing lately.

"I was just trying to decide which one to read first," she replied. Resting on Gaylynn's lap was something old and something new. The something new was a book Hunter had given her; the something old was a book of Gypsy folk tales that her parents had read to her when she'd been growing up.

Gaylynn had asked her mom to send it down to her. She vividly remembered how her mother had faithfully kept to the lines of the storybook, while her father had always elaborated and made up his own version of the story as he went along.

Looking at the table of contents, Gaylynn recognized so many of her childhood favorites—"The Bottle of Brains" being one of them. But for this first session she read them "The Golden Pear" about a sick king and his four sons and a magical Gypsy who told them to search for the golden pear that would cure him.

The tale was a big hit. She followed that folk story with a Cherokee one—"Why the Possum's Tail Is Bare"—from a book donated by Hunter, who had read the story to her the night before. Her attention wandered momentarily as she dreamily recalled how, after Hunter finished reading, they'd started "making out," as he'd put it, in front of the fireplace at his cabin.

"Aren't you gonna read?" one of the children asked her with another tug on her skirt.

"Right." And so she started reading the story, which talked about the dangers of vanity. "In days almost forgotten, the Possum had a beautiful, bushy tail that he was so proud of he would comb it every morning and brag about it. So much so that The Rabbit, who had no tail since the Bear pulled it out, became very jealous. He made up his mind to play a trick on Possum."

The story was short, just the right length for the group of six-year-olds' attention span. They were all laughing by the time she'd finished up by saying, "And afterward Possum was so surprised and ashamed that he could not say a word. Instead, he rolled over helpless on the ground and grinned as Possum does to this day when surprised."

After Gaylynn had checked out a book to each child, she put the records in the wooden box that had been in use since the library's opening days. She'd already typed up eighteen library cards on the old Remington typewriter that was an antique and was missing the letter Z. Luckily, no one had a Z in their name so she'd managed.

There was no money to buy new books, but the collection, especially the children's books, seemed like a solid one. She added the idea of writing out a grant application to her increasing mental list of things to do.

Once the children were gone, Gaylynn was alone in the building—aside from Boone and Stella, who were totally engrossed in each other. Ma Battle had said she'd stop by later to talk about the possibility of holding a literacy class at the library. Gaylynn could talk to her then about applying for private foundation or government grant money to keep the library going.

When Gaylynn reached over for her childhood storybook, a piece of paper fluttered to the floor. Apparently, it had been stuck in the back of the book.

Picking it up, she read it. "Fear impoverishes, while the acceptance of sorrow can enrich."

The powerful words hit home. It was a Rom saying—she didn't know how she knew that, but she did. And it was certainly one that applied to her. When she'd fled from Chicago, she'd been emotionally impoverished by her fear.

The simple beauty and steadfast presence of the mountains had replenished her soul. Along with that had come gradual peace of mind, and a sad acceptance of Duane's death without the horrible weight of guilt and responsibility Gaylynn had felt before.

"Fear impoverishes," she whispered, tracing the words with her fingertips. How had this piece of paper gotten into the book?

Her fingers strayed from the paper to the ribboned medallion she'd taken to wearing every day. Her smile went from reflective to appreciative as she remembered gaining courage from the medallion to seduce Hunter. In the end, it had been unclear who had been the seducer and who seducee—instead, it had been a mutual expression of passion.

On Gaylynn's part, it had also been an expression of love.

Her gaze strayed over to Boone and Stella, who were shelving books in the nonfiction section. Actually, there was more whispering than working going on.

"Boone Twitty, you get your sorry self out here!" Gaylynn heard Floyd shout so loudly that even Bo Regard, who was lying across the threshold, jerked and paid attention. In fact, the bloodhound hightailed it into the library and hid under a reading table!

Getting up, Gaylynn went to see what all the commotion was about. She didn't have to wait long. Floyd came barreling into the building. Or at least he tried to. So did another man, younger but equally as broad in the beam as Floyd. The result being that both men bounced off the doorframe and had to start again. They ended up bursting into the room like a cork pulled from a bottle.

"Uh-oh, trouble's a'brewin'," Gaylynn murmured like a native.

Nine

"**G**et yer hands off my daughter!" Otis Rue bellowed. At least, Gaylynn assumed it was Otis Rue, Stella's father, because although she'd only seen the man from a distance he was obviously glaring at his only daughter.

"It's plain as the rings on a coon's tail that yer daughter has her hands all over my grandson!" Floyd shouted at Otis.

A brief but fiery shouting match ensued.

Putting two fingers in her mouth, Gaylynn let out an ear-piercing whistle that she'd perfected over the years. It had always quieted a classroom full of even the most obstreperous fourth-graders on the first day of school. It had the same effect on the two grown men. Silence suddenly prevailed.

"Now everybody just calm down and tell me what all this mayhem is about," Gaylynn ordered.

"It's just another sign that those troublemaking Rues are up to no good," Floyd declared.

"It's the Montgomeries who are the troublemakers," Otis flared.

"So this is a feud thing, huh?" Gaylynn said.

The two older men stared at her as if she'd grown two heads.

She stared right back. "Listen, you two, I hate to be the one to break it to you, but we're rapidly approaching the twenty-first century here."

"What does that have to do with anything?" Floyd demanded.

Gaylynn wasn't exactly sure, but it had gotten the two men to momentarily stop shouting at each other.

"It has a great deal to do with things," she continued, momentarily stalling for time as she gathered her thoughts together. "The time has come for this ridiculous feud to stop."

"Are you calling our feud ridiculous?" Otis demanded, his anger now extending to her.

Floyd looked at her with equal irritation. "Our feud is not ridiculous!"

"Okay, bad choice of words," Gaylynn allowed. "But however you describe it, this feud between your two families has got to stop."

"Why's that?"

"Because it's hurting the very people you claim to be trying to protect. Stella and Boone."

"You've only been in town a few weeks and now you're claiming to be an expert on my grandson?" Floyd said. "When pigs fly!"

"Soaring swine is not the issue here," Gaylynn stated in her best teacher's voice. "Neither Stella nor Boone has done anything wrong."

"Not in yer eyes maybe..."

"Do you both want to risk loosing the next generation?" Gaylynn demanded bluntly. "Is that what you want to happen here? Because it will. Boone and Stella can leave Lonesome Gap, like so many other young people have before them. They can move to Ashville or any number of other cities, and have another life there. Do you really want that? Don't you think enough people have left Lonesome Gap? Isn't it time you tried to make more people want to stay here rather than driving them away?"

Floyd and Otis both started shuffling their feet and Gaylynn knew she had them dead to rights.

"Listen, I know all about feuds," she assured them. "Trust me, nobody feuds better than the Rom."

"Don't know them," Floyd declared. "Are they from around these parts?"

"The Rom is another word for Gypsies and in my family's case they're from Hungary. Before you two men so rudely burst in here, I was reading some of their folk stories to the children earlier. There's a folk story, if you will, my family tells about a feud between two rival Gypsy tribes and a charmed magical box that made the two youngest members of the tribe fall in love with each other. With their marriage, the feud ended."

"Are you saying Boone and Stella aim on getting married?" Both men roared in unison.

"*Yes!*" Boone and Stella roared right back, speaking up for the first time.

The two older men were so surprised that their mouths dropped open.

"Now as Gaylynn here says, we can either stay here in town and share our lives with you, or we can leave and start a new life somewhere else. What's it gonna be?" Boone demanded with newfound courage.

"Why...I..." Otis sputtered.

"Well...you..." Floyd stuttered.

"Congratulations, everyone!" Gaylynn said, hugging both now speechless men. "I think you made the right decision. I could tell you were both wise men the first time I met you." She pumped each man's hand in a hearty handshake. "Only wise men would be brave enough to set aside the dictates of the past and make their own decisions."

"What in tarnation is she talking about?" Otis asked Floyd.

"Danged if I know. You know how these city folks are."

"What's going on in here?" Hunter demanded from the doorway. "I got a call saying there was a disturbance at the library."

"Not a disturbance, an engagement," Gaylynn announced.

"Yeah, Hunter," Floyd said with a thump on Hunter's back. "Congratulate us. It appears we just ended the feud."

Only after they'd left—Floyd and Otis along with Boone and Stella—to head over to both Hazel's Hash House and the Lonesome Café with the good news, did Gaylynn realize the personal importance of what had just happened. Despite all the shouting and anger, Gaylynn hadn't panicked. She'd shouted right back, just like her old self. She felt so proud of herself she thought she'd burst!

"Care to explain what just went on in here?" Hunter inquired dryly.

"Magic."

"That's one way of putting it. I never thought the day would come when I'd see those two in the same room together without a shouting match."

"Oh, there was a shouting match," she acknowledged blithely. "I just made sure *I* won it."

"And how did you do that?"

Lifting her chin, she said, "You forget, Hunter, I'm accustomed to dealing with obstreperous children."

"Is that how you'd describe Floyd and Otis?"

"If the shoe fits..."

To her surprise, Hunter leaned over and kissed her. Each of his kisses was unique and this one was no exception. It fiercely expressed his pride and passion.

"What was that for?" she asked unsteadily.

"For being you."

"Hunter, I can't believe you're being such a scaredy-cat about this!"

"All I said was are you sure you know what you're doing?"

"Are you or are you not the man who asked me to cut his hair for him?"

"That was before I saw that gleam in your eyes when you have a pair of scissors in your hand."

"I won't cut off anything...necessary," she said with a sassy grin and a naughty swipe at his lap.

Seconds later, after first making sure he placed the scissors safely on the table, he tumbled her into his lap to nuzzle her earlobe. "Yer gonna pay for that, woman!" he growled in his best mountain-man voice.

"I most certainly hope so," she replied, her demure voice at odds with the sassy expectation of her smile. "What exactly did you have in mind?"

"A little of this—" he nuzzled her neck with his lips "—a lot of that." He slid his hand up her bare leg. The cutoffs she was wearing allowed him plenty of leeway.

"You're just trying to distract me so I won't cut your hair," she claimed breathlessly.

"Is it working?"

"Yes. Everything appears to be working just fine," she replied, provocatively running a fingertip down the placket of his jeans. "Of course, I'd have to examine things more closely to make sure."

"Be my guest," he said, loosening his hold on her to lean back in the chair. "Examine all you want."

"Right after I finish trimming your hair," she declared as, in a flash, she leapt up.

With a plaintive "mrrrow" Blue reminded them of her presence on the other dining room chair. The cross-eyed kitten was watching their every move, eagerly waiting for an opportunity to play. Gaylynn snatched the scissors away just in time, as the kitten had been eyeing them mischievously.

"Why are you so gung ho on cutting my hair?" Hunter demanded.

"You asked me to, remember? Besides, the good women of Lonesome Gap have been giving you the eye much too often lately. You look entirely too sexy."

Rolling his eyes in a dramatic display of martyrdom, he said, "Why do I see a crew cut in my future?"

"Nothing so drastic. Just a snip here. And a snip there." Actually, Gaylynn spent more time running her fingers through his hair than actually cutting it. When push came to shove she didn't have the heart to cut much off. Just a trim so his hair didn't hide his collar as much as it did before. And in the process she got to enjoy the things only a woman in love would appreciate, like the location of every gray hair. She counted thirty-five, most around his temples. "They make you look distinguished," she told him after giving him the exact count.

"I think you gave me another five gray hairs when you came at me with those scissors," he righteously maintained.

"Don't move or I might cut off something I shouldn't," she said as he shifted in his seat while dueling with Blue, using a pencil as a sword. The kitten loved this particular game, it was one Hunter played with her often.

In fact, all the cats had lost their initial fear of him and had been completely won over by him, just as Gaylynn was. Judging from the loudness of their purrs when he petted them, Cleo and her two kittens thought Hunter was the best thing since canned tuna. Gaylynn had to agree. There wasn't a better petter on the face of the earth than Hunter. With that thought in mind, she hurriedly finished up.

"There, all done." She produced a hand mirror with a flourish. "Ta-dah!"

He barely glanced at his reflection. "Very nice. Now I do believe there's the matter of an inspection to take care of?"

"An inspection?"

"Examination may have been the word you used. To make sure everything was in working order," he reminded her.

"Oh, that."

"Yes, that."

"I don't believe you've had the chance to really appreciate what I've got in the bedroom."

"Now that's an offer I can't refuse."

Taking him by the hand she led him to her room. "Notice anything different?"

"The box of condoms on the bedside table is open."

"Besides that." The look she gave him made him think of those TV game shows where the clock was ticking down until you gave the right answer.

"Okay, I confess. Whenever I'm in this room I'm not paying attention to the decor. I'm paying attention to you."

"I know. And I love you for it." She tossed the words out teasingly, fondly, knowing he wouldn't take them seriously even though she meant them that way. "But look around. Surely you notice something different?"

He hurriedly surveyed the room. The white iron bedstead was the same. She'd added dainty feminine touches around the room since moving in—a mirror here, a vase of flowers there, the frilly curtains on the window. She'd turned the cabin into a home instead of just a place to crash. He did recognize the purple floral wreath that she'd asked his opinion about at the shop in town. He didn't recognize...

"The white bed ruffle thing?" he guessed.

"No, that was there before."

"What about that picture?" He pointed to the needlepointed teddy bear holding a quilt—above which were the words When Life Gives You Scraps, Make Quilts.

"You're getting closer," she said, "but no cigar."

"I give up."

"The star quilt. I bought it from Ma Battle this morning. It's beautiful, isn't it?" she noted in admiration, running her hand over the purple-and-white design.

"It's beautiful. Let's break it in." Without further ado, Hunter tumbled her onto the bed.

To his surprise, instead of melting in his arms the way she usually did, Gaylynn bounced right back up. What's more, she yanked him off the bed, too.

"You don't sit on this!" she exclaimed in horror. "It's a piece of art!"

"Then it should be on a wall, not the bed."

"You think so? That's a good idea. I've seen those quilt hangers that can go on the wall. In fact, Ma Battle might have some down at the store. We'll go look now."

"Later. Right now this piece of art is in the way and there are other things I'd rather look at," he noted, giving her a potently intimate look. "Here take this—" He handed her the two end corners of the quilt before going to the head of the bed and taking the other two corners in hand. "We'll fold it nice and pretty," he drawled teasingly, kissing her as he handed over his two corners in the folding process. His lips were gone before she could respond. The devilish gleam in his eyes told her he was taking pleasure in baiting her.

Two could play at that game, she decided. So after he'd bent over to gather up the bottom of the quilt for another fold, she was ready for him. When he straightened, she kissed him just as he had her—kamikaze fashion, there and gone.

"You pick up fast," he noted with a smile of appreciation.

"So do you," she replied, for she'd no sooner turned to put the neatly folded quilt over the ladderback chair in the corner than he'd managed to undo the buttons on the back of her blouse.

This time when he tumbled her onto the bed, she welcomed him with open arms. And as they made love she told herself that this was enough, that the words didn't matter, the feeling did.

"You're not peeking, are you?" Hunter demanded as he slowly guided Gaylynn past a thick rhododendron bush. It was mid-May and the buds hadn't blossomed yet, but when they did splashes of color would garnish this little-known walking path. He kept her pressed close, as if he were her shadow.

"How can I peek when you've got your giant hands across my eyes?" Gaylynn retorted.

"I only have *one* hand across your eyes," Hunter reminded her. "The other one is guiding you."

Nominally, his outstretched hand rested on her shoulder, but every third step or so it would slide lower until his little finger rested on the curve of her breast.

"I know where you're *guiding* me, all right," she retorted. "Down the garden path! Are we going to see any *trillium erectum* today?" she naughtily inquired.

"Maybe. If you're lucky. Okay, now are you ready?"

"Umm," she murmured. "And it feels like you are, too," she noted saucily, wiggling her fanny against him.

He paid her back by lowering his hand from her eyes to cup her breast. "There. What do you think?"

"Mmm!" Keeping her eyes closed, she leaned her head back to rest on his chest. "Very nice!"

Bending his head, he whispered in her ear. "I meant the view."

"Oh." Her eyes snapped open. "Right."

The sound of rushing water had warned her that they were near a river. But only now did she realize that they were also in front of a waterfall bracketed by lush greenery. The sun glinted off the dancing water, creating sparkling threads of diamonds. Water leapt over the rocks with frothy abandonment before going over the sharp edge and falling with sheer exuberance. The trembling rush of sound made wonderful music.

"It's beautiful," she breathed. "How did you find this place? I mean, it seems completely hidden away up here."

"It is. It's my special place. I come here to get away from everything."

Gaylynn set down the picnic basket she'd been carrying before turning in his loose embrace to throw her arms around his neck and kiss him.

"What was that for?" he asked against her mouth, even as he kept nibbling her lower lip.

"Be bing be beer," she mumbled back without removing her mouth from his.

"Be bing be beer?" he repeated with a laugh.

She leaned away to translate. "For bringing me here. I *love* it." Her voice reflected her love for him, as well, a love she couldn't say aloud for fear of driving him away. The past few weeks had been picture perfect, with Hunter spending every spare moment with her. His deputy, Charlie, had recovered completely from the gunshot wound in his foot and was able to resume his normal share of the work, which left Hunter with more time for Gaylynn.

She'd scheduled her volunteer time at the library to coincide with his work hours, which left her free to take off with him whenever the opportunity arose. He'd even driven her along the Blue Ridge Parkway as he'd wanted to do from the first day she'd arrived. And she'd kissed him at every scenic pull-off, and the parkway had plenty of scenic pull-offs.

Today the weather had turned quite hot and sultry, but here by the waterfall it was very pleasant. When Hunter had first told her that they'd be walking from his cabin to this secret picnic ground, she hadn't been sure that the red shirt and lightweight denim skirt she wore were the proper attire for hiking. After all, the woods did have their share of poison ivy in them.

She'd wanted to change clothes, but Hunter had assured her that the walk they'd be taking was danger-free. "Aside from me," he'd added with a lusty look at her bare legs. "And I may prove to be very dangerous indeed."

He was right. A simple look from him was dangerous, because it made her heart skip and her hopes take flight. This was their first picnic together. She felt like a teenager again.

"M'lady..." Gallantly taking her hand, Hunter lowered her to the red-and-white checked tablecloth he'd set out on the sun-drenched top of a flat boulder.

He'd brought plenty of finger food. Bite-size chunks of Swiss cheese and honey-cured ham. Grapes. Tiny corncobs. And oranges. Ah, the oranges! She'd never have guessed what a seductive use he'd put them to.

She'd started out fascinated by the strength of his hands as he'd peeled away the outer rind. She sat in the open V of his legs, her back against his chest. He'd peeled the orange in front of her, his arms around her so that she could feel the movement of his muscles as he ripped the fruit's outer flesh away to reveal the tender inner delicacy. Breaking it into segments, he brought a piece up to her mouth, inviting her to take a bite. She did. It was a very juicy orange. She found out just how juicy when he drizzled the dripping juice down her shirtfront by accident. Or so he claimed.

"I'll clean that up right away," he promised her, shifting her so that she lay across his lap, resting against the crook of his arm. Bending his head, he licked the sweet juice from her warm skin in an erotic trail from her collarbone down to the slope of her breast.

It proved to be such a delightful clean-up operation that he just had to drizzle more orange juice—drip by drip, lick by lick. Squeezing the orange slice, squeezing her breast in the palm of his hand.

"I better get your shirt out of the way before it gets more juice on it," he noted, expertly removing the article of clothing.

She wore a lacy cotton tank top underneath, the stretchy material acting as her only bra. Hunter drew in a shaky breath. He could see the dusky areolas of her nipples through the lacework.

He went to lift that final piece of lingerie out of his way, as well, but her hand on his wrist stopped him. "Anyone could see us out here!"

"No one comes up here." He grinned wickedly before adding, "Although I'm about to make sure that we both come. If you don't feel comfortable right here, there is someplace else."

She scrambled to grab her shirt as he slid her off his lap and stood. "Leave the stuff here," he said, taking her hand and hauling her up beside him. He kissed her, the forceful pressure declaring his fierce need for her. "Come on," he growled, heading straight for the waterfall.

"I can't swim, just in case you were thinking of
dunking me," she warned him.

"No dunking, no swimming, although there will be
some submerging and mutual drowning going on. But
in passion, not water. Be careful, the rock is wet and
slippery here." He kept his arm around her waist pro-
tectively.

"Are there bears in there?"

"No, but I hope to get *you* bare in here," he
growled.

Seconds later they were in a hidden grotto behind the
waterfall. The sound of the rushing water pounded
through the air, almost deafening in its intensity. So,
too, was desire pounding through Gaylynn's body, almost deafening her in its intensity.

She didn't care that the grotto was small, that the air
was damp and cool. His lips were enough to warm her,
to start a fire that only his complete possession could
put out. He guided her over to a wide rock formation
at the back of the grotto. It elevated her to the perfect
height for him. Sliding his hand behind her knee, he
lifted her leg. Two long, wet, tongue-tangling kisses
later, her full skirt was bunched up around her waist
and her panties had miraculously disappeared. His
jeans and underwear were lowered, allowing his arousal
to spring free.

The grotto wall at her back was slippery and cool, his
body was hard and hot. Protection was taken care of
and then, gripping her bent knee and lifting it once
again so that she was positioned just right, he joined
with her, the darkly erotic probing extending his full
possession as he slowly moved deeper—inch by joyous
inch. The blunt tip, the throbbing thickness,

more... more... then the complete width and breadth of him.

"Ahh." Her moan of pleasure was felt rather than heard by either one of them.

He slid even farther into her.

"Yes!"

Buried in her welcoming depths, he kissed her, the thrust of his tongue mimicking each seductive thrust elsewhere. Starting out slowly, almost leisurely, Hunter rocked against her. Adding a twist here, a shift there. Rubbing against her with excruciating sureness. Withdrawing only to slide forward again, creating pleasure so intense it was almost painful.

The life force of the waterfall tumultuously pounded in the background even as she tightened around him. Digging her fingers into his shoulders, she panted his name as the first delicate shudders of ecstasy took hold—rippling, rolling, swelling—wave after wave cascading through her.

She reached the apex, poised on the pinnacle of rapture when he thrust into her and stiffened in her arms. Hunter threw back his head and shouted. Then she was pitching over the other side, tumbling in a free fall from bliss.

Afterward, mere words couldn't express the enormity of what they'd just shared. Uncaring of the effect on her skirt, she sat down on the rock formation. He sat beside her.

"Wow," she whispered unsteadily. Her feelings were so intense, so laid-out-there-for-him-to-see that she instinctively tried to defuse the moment by using humor. "Come here often?" she wickedly asked him.

"You've got a naughty mouth," he replied appreciatively.

Before they left the grotto, she showed him just how naughty her mouth could be.

Whack! The sharp ax sliced another chunk of wood into halves. With every swing, the muscles along Hunter's back and arms rippled in unison. Sitting on a stump nearby, Gaylynn had the best seat in the house.

They'd returned from the sensual picnic at the waterfall a short while ago and Hunter had decided that he wanted to build a fire in the fireplace that night.

"No one builds better fires than you," she'd complimented him, nibbling on his earlobe the way he so often had on hers. She was delighted to discover that he was just as sensitive that way as she was.

"Are you one of them fast city women tryin' to lead a poor mountain boy astray?" he demanded in pretended moral outrage.

"I'm doin' mah best," she drawled in an imperfect impersonation of a Southern belle.

"Then here, take the picnic basket inside and bring me a drink while I chop us up some wood."

"Oh, yes, mountain man," she said with mocking acquiescence. "Shall I make you a peanut-butter-and-banana sandwich while I'm in the kitchen?"

"No, but a peanut-butter-and-ketchup one would be great about now."

"In your dreams," she retorted as she marched up the steps to his cabin, making sure to add as much swing to her walk as possible. She noticed that her provocative action had not gone unnoticed by Hunter.

He gave a long and loud wolf call followed by a whistle. "You've got legs like a Tennessee walkin' horse," he drawled.

"Meaning what, that they're short?" she demanded, being totally unfamiliar with equine anatomy.

"Meaning they're shapely."

"Oh. In that case, thank you kindly," she said with a sassy smile and a seductive flip of her skirt.

"Don't forget that drink," he reminded her. "And could you bring me a towel while you're in there? A man could work up a proper sweat chopping wood."

She envisioned nothing *proper* about a shirtless, sweat-slickened Hunter.

And now here she was, sitting front row center, watching him work. Every so often, he'd pause and take a cooling sip of the beer she'd brought out for him.

She'd chosen lemonade for herself, figuring that ogling him would be intoxicating enough.

Now, as Hunter leaned back his head to take a slow sip of beer straight from the can, she watched the ripple of his throat as he swallowed. His jeans hung low on his hips, displaying his muscular torso.

Mine, she thought to herself with a wickedly feminine sense of power. All mine!

But for how long? an inner voice niggled in her ear. Hunter never talked about the future. They'd shared moments more intimate than she'd ever dreamed possible. And not just physically, but emotionally, as well. And while there were moments when she thought she could read his every thought, there were many more times when he remained as much a mystery as ever.

"Hey, coffee break is over," she called out. "Back to work."

"Slave driver," he grumbled as he crunched the empty aluminum can in one hand.

"Show off," she retorted fondly.

Afterward, Gaylynn could never say exactly what went wrong. One moment Hunter was laughing at what she'd said, the next his ax slipped, slicing through denim and skin and gashing his thigh wide open.

Ten

Blood. It seemed to be everywhere!

Gaylynn froze, paralyzed by a flashback of the TV news image—the sight of blood on the street plastered all over her TV screen. Duane's blood. Staining the street. Proclaiming his death.

But it was Hunter who was bleeding now.

Instinctively touching the ribboned medallion she wore, Gaylynn gained strength from it. The panic instantly cleared and she knew what she had to do.

Galvanized into action, Gaylynn rushed toward him, grabbing the thick towel from the front porch as she did so. Hunter, conscious but shaky, was pressing his hand to his thigh in a vain attempt to staunch the flow of blood. Gently shifting his hand, she placed the towel over the wound and applied a steady pressure. She needed to get him to a hospital fast.

"Is there an ambulance or emergency medivac I can call?"

Hunter shook his head. "Need to drive to Summerville. Hospital...there."

"Okay, that's what we're going to do, then. We'll get to Summerville."

Slipping out of her blouse with one hand, while keeping her other hand pressed to the towel, she heard Hunter weakly mutter, "Much as I'd like to, I don't think I'm up to fooling around right now."

Even now, he was trying to tease her. "Don't talk," she said. "Save your strength."

"Gonna pass out..." he warned her. And he did. She prayed it was because of the sight of all the blood and not because he'd lost so much of it. While he was out she wrapped her shirt around the towel, to hold it in place. Yanking the bandanna she wore in her hair, she used that to firmly tie the makeshift bandage in place.

All the while she remained calm and confident as she did what had to be done. She'd taken first-aid classes; she knew what the drill was. No tourniquet, that would cut off circulation. Steady pressure was best.

Hunter regained consciousness as she finished binding the wound. Now she needed to get him into his car, which thankfully was nearby. But even so, she needed his help getting him into the vehicle.

"Hey, big guy, think you can stay awake long enough to stand up and mosey over to your car?"

"Car keys front pocket...jeans."

Reaching into his pocket, she felt the warmth of his skin through the denim and was struck anew how much she loved him. She couldn't bear seeing him hurt. "Got them."

Catching a glimpse of panic behind her bravado, Hunter apologized, "Sorry about this, Red."

"Hey, I'm not the one who passed out at the sight of a little blood," she joked. "I'm a tough cookie, remember?" Spotting a long, stout branch in the woodpile, she hurriedly brought it over, grabbing his discarded shirt and slipping it on en route. "Do you think you can stand if you use this as a crutch?"

"Sure thing."

It was tricky, but they managed. Draping his arm around her shoulders, she propped him up, using more strength than she thought she had. She'd had the foresight to open the back door of the car before they'd started, so all Hunter had to do was sink onto the back seat and she took care of the rest, carefully easing his leg onto the bench seat as he reclined against the opposite door. Kneeling on the floor mat, she positioned his leg as best she could, fastening a seat belt around his hip to keep him in place should he pass out again.

Gravel flew from the tires as she backed his sheriff's car out of the driveway, turning around in front of his cabin before heading on down the mountain as quickly as she could without making the ride too bumpy for him. Driving with one hand, she used her other hand to activate the cellular phone she had in her purse, calling Floyd at the base of the hill.

"Where's the nearest hospital, Floyd?"

"Over in Summerville. Why?"

"I need help. Is Boone there?"

"No, he took Stella and Ma Battle shopping over in Summerville. He won't be back until later. What's wrong? Did you hurt yourself?"

"Not me, it's Hunter. I'm driving down now—we should be at your place in about ten minutes. I'm going to need you to drive Hunter's car while I'm in the back with him, applying pressure to the wound on his leg."

"I'll be outside ready and waiting," Floyd promised. "Don't you worry none. I'll get us over to Summerville in a jiffy."

Gaylynn was worried plenty. There was so much that could go wrong. "Call the hospital and tell them we're coming in, okay?"

"Will do."

As promised, Floyd was waiting outside, wearing a pair of Coke-bottle glasses. "I hate wearing the doggone things," he grumbled, "but I figured I'd better be able to see. These glasses sure do make a mighty big difference," he noted as he hopped into the car, taking the place behind the steering wheel that Gaylynn had just vacated. The second she was in the back seat, kneeling on the floor, Floyd said, "Now which of these here switches starts the sirens . . . ah, there it is. I always wanted to drive me one of these po-leeese cars," he noted with excitement as he drove onto the road. "I'm mighty obliged to you, Hunter, for giving me the opportunity. Shame that you had to get hurt to do it, though. No offense, Hunter," he assured him, turning his head over his shoulder to give him a quick look. "I didn't mean it that way."

"None taken," Hunter replied, his face pale, the grim line of his lips proclaiming the amount of pain he was in.

"You two just sit tight and I'll have you in Summerville in the wink of a possum's eye," Floyd declared.

Gaylynn knelt on the floor in the back, using both her hands to apply steady pressure to Hunter's bandaged thigh.

"I've always wanted to have a beautiful woman on her knees before me," Hunter muttered.

"You couldn't think of an easier way to get attention?" she questioned with only a slight quiver in her voice.

"At least Floyd gets to fulfill a lifelong dream of driving a sheriff's car."

"Next time just lend him the keys," Gaylynn retorted.

"Sure thing, Red."

He was still shirtless, allowing her to see the shallow rise and fall of his chest as he breathed.

"Are you cold?" she asked in concern. "Do you want your shirt back?"

He shook his head and gripped her shoulder. "Keep it. Don't want . . . any of the doctors . . . eyeing you."

"Trust me, that won't be a problem. It's the nurses eyeing *you* that worries me," she teasingly replied.

"Don't . . . worry."

Easier said than done, she thought to herself even as she kept up a steady prattle of conversation, hoping to reassure them both that Hunter would be fine. She didn't give him time to answer, she just wanted to keep his mind occupied on something other than the burning pain in his thigh. And as she cheerfully babbled away, she was silently praying that he'd be okay, fervently calling on every saint she'd ever heard of and then some.

With sirens blaring and lights flashing, Floyd got them to the hospital in record time. As he'd said, he knew these roads like the back of his hand and the thick glasses he wore apparently did the trick on his "sore" eyes because he had no trouble finding the hospital's emergency room entrance.

Orderlies came rushing out with a gurney, and Hunter was whisked away, out of sight. They wouldn't let Gaylynn stay with him, instead waylaying her to fill out insurance forms. She filled out the lines she could. She didn't know Hunter's social security number, but she did know his mother's maiden name. Handing back the forms, she said, "When can I see him? Is he going to be okay?"

"We'll let you know," a bland-faced nurse replied.

Floyd sat with Gaylynn as she paced the tiny emergency waiting room. Back and forth she went, as nervous as a cat. And all the while thoughts were dashing through her head—flashes of memories, mental snapshots. Hunter with his hand over her eyes, leading her to his secret waterfall. Making love to her in the grotto. Sitting across from her at the Lonesome Café and stealing fries off her plate. Grabbing her around the waist as she peeked into the library's windows. Playing one-on-one basketball with her. Dueling with Blue. Introducing her to his many cousins. Joking with her even when he was in pain on the way to the hospital.

The accident sliced through her futile fears, making her realize how empty her life would be without him. Everything else was just minor stuff, things that could be worked out. She loved him enough for both of them. And she wasn't afraid of anything as much as not having him in her life. Nothing was more terrifying than the thought of losing him.

The small waiting room got even more crowded when Boone, Stella and Ma Battle showed up. "I called home and heard about Hunter's accident," Boone said. "How's he doing?"

"We don't know yet," Gaylynn replied, her voice tense. "They're still treating him."

"Now don't you worry none," Ma Battle said, putting a reassuring arm around Gaylynn's shoulders. "Hunter is as strong as an ox. He'll be just fine, you'll see."

"I hope so," Gaylynn whispered.

"I know this might not be the proper time and all, but I do have some news for you. Good news about those literacy classes I was talking about having at the library. The Ladies Auxiliary League got their quarterly statement in and we done real good on our investing."

"That's nice," Gaylynn said, only half listening.

"So we voted last night and decided to donate part of our profits to a library fund. We come up with a donation totaling fifteen thousand dollars, give or take a thousand here or there."

Boone's and Stella's eyes looked ready to bulge out. It was their astonishment that gradually sank through to Gaylynn and made her concentrate on what Ma Battle had just told her.

"Fifteen thousand dollars?" Boone repeated.

The older woman nodded. "We done real well on those high-tech investments we chose. And on the health-care stocks, too."

"You mean you didn't win a contest or something?" Boone asked.

"No contest, no. For the past six years or so the Ladies Auxiliary League has been investing in stocks. We did the research on the companies and then chose small companies with wonderful growth opportunities that ended up giving us a very high yield and a mighty fine rate of return."

"I thought you gals was just jawin' and quiltin'," Floyd said.

"You thought wrong. We pooled our resources, the money we'd made over the years from our quilts and other things. Land sake's, we made *quite* a killing on Wall Street. Course in the early years we reinvested all our profits to make even bigger gains."

"Well, don't that beat all." Floyd sounded stunned.

"Bessie was going to surprise you and tell you tonight," Ma Battle told Floyd. "But I thought Gaylynn here could use some good news right about now, even though I know there's no news that'll be as good as her hearing that Hunter is going to be okay."

As if on cue, the doctor walked into the waiting room. "You folks here about Hunter Davis?"

"That's right," Gaylynn replied. "How is he?"

"He needed a dozen stitches," the doctor said, "but there was no arterial or tendon damage. He's a very lucky man. You did a good job getting him in here right away and applying that bandage to the wound."

"Can I see him now?" Gaylynn asked.

"Sure thing. The nurse will show you where he is."

Hunter was sitting up in bed, glaring at a nurse who had a needle in one hand. "Get away from me! I've been stabbed and prodded enough for one day." To Gaylynn he said, "They ruined my best pair of jeans. Cut the leg right off!"

"It was either the jeans or *your* leg—one of the two had to go," the middle-aged nurse retorted tartly. "Be glad you're not in worse shape." With a sniff of disapproval she marched out.

"Yes, be glad," Gaylynn agreed as she came to his bedside in the emergency room cubicle. "I know I am. How do you feel?"

"Like I've been hit by an ax."

She held on to his hand as if afraid to let it go.

"How soon can you get me out of here?" he demanded.

"Soon. I've got something to tell you first."

"Can't it wait?"

"No. I... It's... I love you," she blurted out. "Now you may already know this. I've certainly known it for ages. But I need to tell you. I need you to know how important you are to me. I want to spend the rest of my life with you. No, don't say anything yet. I need to get this off my chest. I'm not going to be ruled by fear anymore. I'm not going to let panic prevent me from going after what I want. And I want you. As my husband."

She had to draw in a deep breath before rushing on. "Now you know I had a crush on you when I was a teenager, but this is more than that. If I didn't know that the charmed box didn't work on you, I would almost have said that it was destiny. Heck, it *is* destiny, box or no. So the Gypsy love-charmed box was supposed to make me fall in love with the first man I saw and that man wasn't you—it was some derelict moonshiner walking through the woods by my cabin the first day I arrived. I mean, if you think about it, it's really lucky for me that the love-charmed box turned out to be was just a fanciful legend," she said. "Or I'd have fallen for that guy."

"There are no moonshiners in those woods, derelict or otherwise," he said on the verge of laughter.

"Okay, so maybe he was just some strange old man."

"He wasn't that old."

"How do you know?"

"Because he was me. I mean, *I* was the old guy dressed as a bum. I'd just come off a day's undercover operation at the county seat. Someone was rolling drunk bums and they needed some extra help so I volunteered since I'd done some undercover work up in Chicago. Anyway, I didn't change clothes after the job—I just headed straight up to my cabin."

"But your car... I heard your car drive up later."

"My car overheated," he admitted. "I took a shortcut through the woods to get some water for the radiator. While I was at my cabin, I changed into my regular clothes before walking down again."

"Why didn't you tell me this before? Didn't you see me looking at you? Couldn't you tell you'd startled me?"

"I didn't think you'd seen me. It looked like you were engrossed in something on your lap."

"The box was on my lap. The one you looked at in my cabin, with all the engraving on it, remember?"

"I remember. It's must be made out of some kind of special metal because it's warm to the touch."

"Only when it's working its magic. It was *you* all along! I don't believe this!"

"Then are you going to have a hard time believing I love you?"

"Not at all," she replied with a joyful grin. "Obviously, the charmed Gypsy box has worked its magic again!"

"Not the box, *you.*" He tenderly stroked her cheek with the back of his hand. "*You* worked your magic. On me. I know you've been through a tough time and that I may be taking advantage of your vulnerability—"

"Excuse me," she interrupted him. "Who was the one who saved your leg if not your very life? Me. The way I see it, you owe me big-time, mister!" she stated, tenderly jabbing her finger against his bare chest. "And don't think I'm not going to collect."

"And how do you aim on doing that?"

"Oh, I figure thirty or forty years of marriage should do it," she replied with a gleam in her eye. "For starters."

"Sounds like a fair deal to me," he readily agreed, raising their clasped hands to kiss her fingers. "Starting when?"

"As soon as possible," she declared.

"It can't happen soon enough for me," he said, tugging her down to seal the pledge with a kiss, declaring his love for her more eloquently than mere words could.

Ten days later

"You know, when I made a wish and blew out the candles way back on my sixteenth birthday, this is what I wished for," Gaylynn murmured as she laid in bed, snuggled against his shoulder while admiring the wide gold wedding band on her finger. "To be your wife."

"I sure hope it was worth the wait," Hunter replied, trailing his fingers down her bare arm to entwine them with hers.

"Oh, it definitely was. I'm just glad we decided not to waste any more time and eloped."

"Are you sorry we came back here for our honeymoon?" he asked.

"Not at all. We've got our own honeymoon cabin in the woods here. Your place."

"No heart-shaped tubs, though."

"We don't need any. We've got a grotto hidden behind a waterfall. And you've got remarkable healing capacities, even the doctors said so." The wound on his leg had mended so well that he'd quickly been able to dispense with the walking cane he'd had to use for the first few days after the accident.

"Maybe it's that Gypsy box of yours at work again. There's still a scar on my leg, though."

"So I'll always remember how close I came to losing you. If you'd have been here alone cutting wood . . ."

"But I wasn't."

She nodded and deliberately chased that image out of her head, instead focusing on their surroundings in his bedroom. "You know, it's very handy that the layout of this place is the same as my brother's, right down to the windows. So the priscilla curtains will fit on the window. And of course the quilt—"

"Can hang on the wall," Hunter interrupted her to declare. "No use having something that delicate and fragile on the bed."

"No? You don't think *I'm* delicate and fragile?"

He grinned wolfishly at her. "You have your moments."

"You're too kind."

"And you're too far away." Placing his hand on the back of her head, he tenderly urged it back onto his chest.

"You think my mother is ever going to forgive me for eloping?" she wondered, tracing imaginary circles over the muscular curves of his chest.

"Come on, she didn't sound that upset to me when we talked to her over the phone. And your father claimed he knew this would happen."

Gaylynn raised her head to look into Hunter's eyes. "Yeah, well, you do realize that later this summer we're going to go up there and have a big wedding reception at my parents' house with all my relatives there toasting us with *palinka*."

"And we'll have to have a bash down here with all my cousins," he added. "Floyd can play his fiddle. My folks will fly in from Florida."

"Maybe we shouldn't have told them about eloping."

"And have them think we're just living in sin? No way. Your father might have put a Gypsy curse on me."

"Listen, you've already had a Gypsy curse put on you," she told him with a saucy smile. "You were destined to find love 'where you looked for it...'"

"Don't forget the 'and live happily ever after' part," he reminded her, running his fingertip down her adorable nose.

"You've been reading my folk stories again," she murmured against his warm lips.

"Mmm." He inched his way around her mouth, gliding his tongue over every curve. "But this is fact, not fiction."

"Being this happy should be against the law."

"You're married to the law in this town, so I don't think you have anything to worry about."

Gaylynn *knew* she didn't have anything to worry about. She'd found true love in the heart of the one man in all the world for her. She'd also found a new life as Lonesome Gap's much-needed and much appreciated librarian. She'd experienced the magic, and now it was time to fulfill the rest of the family legend by sending the love-charmed box on to her brother, Dylan. *He won't know what hit him,* was Gaylynn's last thought before she focused all her attention on her new husband.

* * * * *

The box hasn't finished working its magic yet. There's one more Janos to find love. See how Dylan gets roped and wed in Book Three of THREE WEDDINGS AND A GIFT— *ABBIE AND THE COWBOY— coming in November 1996 from Silhouette Desire!*

For the Janos siblings

Three Weddings and a Gift

leads to a lot of loving!
Join award-winning author

Cathie Linz

as she shows how an *unusual* inheritance leads to
love at first sight—and beyond!—in

MICHAEL'S BABY #1023
September 1996

SEDUCING HUNTER #1029
October 1996

and

ABBIE AND THE COWBOY #1036
November 1996

Only from

SILHOUETTE® *Desire*

Take 4 bestselling love stories FREE

Plus get a FREE surprise gift!

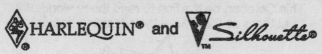

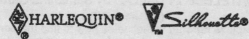 

This October, be the first to read these wonderful authors as they make their dazzling debuts!

Women to Watch

THE WEDDING KISS by Robin Wells
(Silhouette Romance #1185)
A reluctant bachelor rescues the woman he loves
from the man she's about to marry—and turns into
a willing groom himself!

THE SEX TEST by Patty Salier
(Silhouette Desire #1032)
A pretty professor learns there's more to making love
than meets the eye when she takes lessons from
a sexy stranger.

IN A FAMILY WAY by Julia Mozingo
(Special Edition #1062)
A woman without a past finds shelter in the arms of
a handsome rancher. Can she trust him to protect
her unborn child?

UNDER COVER OF THE NIGHT by Roberta Tobeck
(Intimate Moments #744)
A rugged government agent encounters the woman he has
always loved. But past secrets could threaten their future.

DATELESS IN DALLAS by Samantha Carter
(Yours Truly)
A hapless reporter investigates how to find the perfect
mate—and winds up falling for her handsome rival!

Don't miss the brightest stars of tomorrow!

Only from ▼ *Silhouette*®
™

The collection of the year!
NEW YORK TIMES BESTSELLING AUTHORS

Linda Lael Miller
Wild About Harry

Janet Dailey
Sweet Promise

Elizabeth Lowell
Reckless Love

Penny Jordan
Love's Choices

and featuring
Nora Roberts
The Calhoun Women

This special trade-size edition features four of the wildly
popular titles in the Calhoun miniseries together in
one volume—a true collector's item!

Pick up these great authors and a chance to win
a weekend for two in New York City at the
Marriott Marquis Hotel on Broadway! We'll pay
for your flight, your hotel—even a Broadway show!

Available in December at your favorite retail outlet.

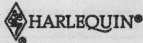 

As seen on TV!
Free Gift Offer

With a Free Gift proof-of-purchase from any Silhouette® book,
you can receive a beautiful cubic zirconia pendant.

This gorgeous marquise-shaped stone is a genuine cubic
zirconia—accented by an 18" gold tone necklace.

(Approximate retail value $19.95)

Send for yours today...
compliments of ▼ *Silhouette®*

To receive your free gift, a cubic zirconia pendant, send us one original proof-of-
purchase, photocopies not accepted, from the back of any Silhouette Romance™,
Silhouette Desire®, Silhouette Special Edition®, Silhouette Intimate Moments®
or Silhouette Yours Truly™ title available in August, September or October at your favorite
retail outlet, together with the Free Gift Certificate, plus a check or money order for
$1.65 U.S./$2.15 CAN. (do not send cash) to cover postage and handling, payable
to Silhouette Free Gift Offer. We will send you the specified gift. Allow 6 to 8 weeks for
delivery. Offer good until October 31, 1996 or while quantities last. Offer valid in the
U.S. and Canada only.

Free Gift Certificate

Name: _____

Address: _____

City: _____ State/Province: _____ Zip/Postal Code: _____

Mail this certificate, one proof-of-purchase and a check or money order for postage
and handling to: SILHOUETTE FREE GIFT OFFER 1996. In the U.S.: 3010 Walden
Avenue, P.O. Box 9077, Buffalo NY 14269-9077. In Canada: P.O. Box 613, Fort Erie,
Ontario L2Z 5X3.

FREE GIFT OFFER   084-KMD
ONE PROOF-OF-PURCHASE
To collect your fabulous FREE GIFT, a cubic zirconia pendant, you must include this
original proof-of-purchase for each gift with the properly completed Free Gift Certificate.

084-KMD

SILHOUETTE®

Desire

He's tough enough to capture your heart,
Tender enough to cradle a newborn baby
And sexy enough to satisfy your wildest fantasies....

He's Silhouette Desire's MAN OF THE MONTH!

From the moment he meets the woman of his
dreams to the time the handsome hunk says *I do*...

Fall in love with these incredible men:

In July: *THE COWBOY AND THE KID*
                by Anne McAllister

In August: *DON'T FENCE ME IN*
                by Kathleen Korbel

In September: *TALLCHIEF'S BRIDE*
                by Cait London

In October: *THE TEXAS BLUE NORTHER*
                by Lass Small

In November: *STRYKER'S WIFE*
                by Dixie Browning

In December: *CHRISTMAS PAST*
                by Joan Hohl

MAN OF THE MONTH...ONLY FROM
SILHOUETTE DESIRE

MOM96JD

You're About to Become a

Privileged Woman

Reap the rewards of fabulous free gifts and
benefits with proofs-of-purchase from
Silhouette and Harlequin books

Pages & Privileges™

It's our way of thanking you for
buying our books at your
favorite retail stores.

PROOF OF PURCHASE
Offer expires October 31, 1996

SD-PP180

Harlequin and Silhouette—
the most privileged readers in the world!

For more information about Harlequin and
Silhouette's PAGES & PRIVILEGES program call the
Pages & Privileges Benefits Desk: 1-503-794-2499

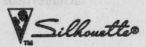

SD-PP180